CRUSOE BOYS

VINCENT SERVENTY

Matt and Tom were off on the adventure of their lives! Sailing to an island of their own, exploring unknown territory, setting up house, living off the land, having adventures and, for a time, all by themselves.

Wasn't that every one's dream? They could be Crusoe boys, with no school, no clocks, no rules ...

But — the storm, illness, then the bad news ... It almost turned into a chilling nightmare.

Cover painting by Andrew Lewis.

Vincent Serventy, the youngest of a large family, spent his early years on a lonely farm in the hills of Bickley near Perth. The children ran wild like brumbies through the bush, a world filled with birdsong and, in spring, alive with a mass of wildflowers.

In later years, after attending schools nearer the city and finally university, he began travels which took him to many parts of the world. Always the thread of Australian wild places tugged him home. He has spent many happy months on islands researching seabirds, his most loved field of natural history. Many of his own experiences he has distilled into the story, *Crusoe Boys*.

The wildlife the 'Crusoe boys' saw can still be seen today, because the islands are reserves, fragments of the wild saved for all time. Their adventures with sealers and whalers could have happened to boys of the time who ran away for excitement, usually to return sadder and wiser. Matt and Tom were lucky in the friends who cared for them.

Sometimes Vincent wonders what is real and what is fiction in this book. It could have happened ...

Photograph: Ben Smith.

CRUSOE
BOYS

CRUSOE
BOYS

VINCENT SERVENTY

ILLUSTRATIONS BY ANDREW LEWIS

FREMANTLE ARTS CENTRE PRESS

First published 1995 by
FREMANTLE ARTS CENTRE PRESS
193 South Terrace (PO Box 320), South Fremantle
Western Australia 6162.

Consultant Editor Alwyn Evans.
Designed by John Douglass.
Production Coordinator Linda Martin.

Typeset in 12 on 13.4pt Goudy Oldstyle
by Fremantle Arts Centre Press.
and printed on 100 gsm Master Offset
by Scott Four Colour Print, Western Australia.

National Library of Australia
Cataloguing-in-publication data

Serventy, Vincent, 1925 - .
  Crusoe boys.

  ISBN 1 86368 120 5.

  I. Title.

A823.3

Department for
theArts

Western Australia

The State of Western Australia has made an investment in this project
through the Department for the Arts.

This book is dedicated to
the two Andrews boys, long dead, who
lived for a time as all true children would
love to have lived, as untrammelled as
the original Robinson Crusoe.

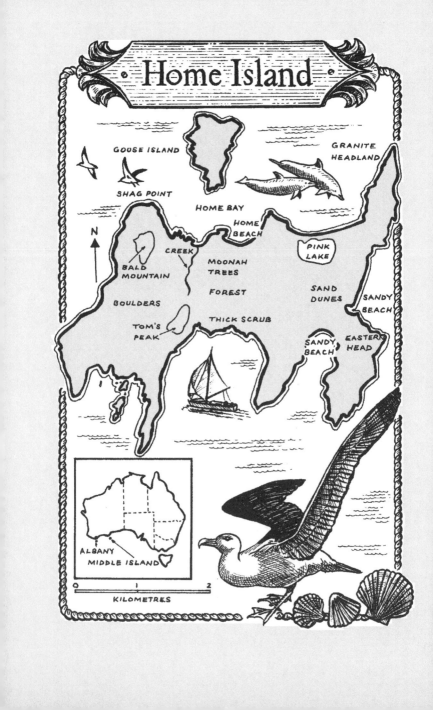

Home Island

GOOSE ISLAND

SHAG POINT

GRANITE HEADLAND

HOME BAY

HOME BEACH

N

CREEK

PINK LAKE

BALD MOUNTAIN

MOONAH TREES

BOULDERS

FOREST

SAND DUNES

SANDY BEACH

TOM'S PEAK

THICK SCRUB

SANDY BEACH

EASTERN HEAD

ALBANY

MIDDLE ISLAND

0   1   2
KILOMETRES

chapter one

THE DEPARTURE

'Ted's a loony, taking those kids to an island at the ends of the earth.' The speaker turned to the bar. 'Two more beers, Ben.'

The group paused in their drinking to watch Ted Somers and his two boys loading a boat at the wharf.

'And Matt's only twelve. Tom fourteen. Ted can look after himself but what about the kids? And no woman. They'll be at each other's throats before the six months is up, you mark my words.'

'Or starve to death,' said another man gloomily.

'Bloody Ted Somers was always a hard man. Since Ann died he's been worse. Have you ever seen him smile?'

The publican leaned over the bar to look at the boat.

'Ah well, a man can always dream. Not a bad idea to leave Albany. Nothing much here these days. Ted can make a new start on Middle Island. It's a long way off and a lonely godforsaken spot they tell me. It needs a hard man to survive. Ted came out with the convict ship in '61 as a warder. He was one of the toughest. You had to be hard, it was no picnic. Some of them lags were real animals. Murder you if they got half a chance.'

'Hold it.' A burly figure turned threateningly to the publican. 'The lot that came to Western Australia were a good crowd. Lags you call them, but they had enough guts to steal food instead of letting their families starve, unlike the rest of the lily-livered workers in England. And some were Fenians like my brother. He fought for Ireland, but was caught by the English and sent to the other side of the earth. The English let our family starve and I won't forget that!' The man turned and spat on the sawdust-covered floor. 'So shut your trap about convicts. Most of us have the blood of lags running in our veins. It's a lot redder than those bloody gentlemen who came out here to make money.'

'Squatters!' continued another man. 'North of Perth they have a dance every night in the new hall we all built. And they have a chalk mark across the middle of it. Gentlefolk on one side of the line, the likes of you and me on the other. But, I've been thinking ...'

A chorus of laughs greeted this remark. 'Good old Bert. The only thinking he's done for years is where he can grab a free beer.'

'Hold your jaw. I tell you the convicts were the lucky ones. What is there in England for the likes of us? Here you can always get a good feed – meat.'

The group was quiet. Bert was right. None of them wanted to go back. Australia was home now.

Bert went on. 'Let me tell you a story about a wee lass. Came out on the same ship as my own grandmother. A pretty girl she was. Stole a horse. Lucky not to have been hanged and her family not lifting a finger to save her. She was clever. Spoke well in the dock and the gentry liked the look of her. She married in Sydney. A ship's captain. Mary Reiby she became. When he died she kept the business. Made a fortune! My gran told me how Mary went back to her old village with her two daughters — all dolled up and very grand in their big coach. Showed her relations that they could whistle for any money from her.'

'You're right Bert. But Ted Somers did all right too. Saved his money and bought a small boat. That was how he started. Now he's the best trader along the coast. The way he's going he could be the biggest soon. But it was a sad day when he lost Ann. She kept him human.'

'Yes,' chimed in another drinker. 'No rubbish in the stock he takes out to the farms along the coast. That *Silver Gull* is a beauty. Could run across the Bight easy. Go around the world she could.'

'Needs to be good,' growled Ben. 'It's a savage coast. You wouldn't catch me out in those seas in the winter. The roaring forties they call those winds. They've blown many a good ship to Davy Jones' locker. But now Ann's dead I suppose Ted wants to forget Albany. The boy Tom's a chip off the old block. Surly like his dad, but he's got guts. As good as a man when it comes to work. Young Matt's a live one though. I feel real sorry for him. With schooling he could go far.'

'Ted's a shrewd judge,' broke in one of the men. 'Middle Island's got a good harbour, plenty of game, and fresh water. Was a whaler's camp once, 'til all the whales were killed.'

Ted and his two boys were still loading the boat.

'We're taking Spot!' Matt spoke firmly.

'Of course,' replied his father. 'He'll be useful. You need a good dog in the bush. And he'll be company for you.'

'For me, too,' complained Tom. 'He's as much mine as Matt's.'

The fox terrier looked from one to the other, ears pricked.

'Yes,' said Somers shortly. 'He'll help catch wallabies and kill snakes.'

'Snakes?' asked Matt.

'Not to worry,' replied his father. 'You know how to kill snakes don't you? I've made a snake killer out of twisted heavy gauge fencing wire. You can hang it near the door. A good whack on the body and that's the finish of the snake. Don't use a stick, that'll just break and bruise the snake. Make it angry. It could still strike.'

'Don't worry, Dad,' said Tom, with his two-year superiority, 'I'll look after Matt.'

Somers gave one of his rare laughs.

'Right. Now for the rest of the cargo. First for the guns. Matt, you hand them to Tom as I call them out. Five pounds of shot, two boxes of caps, two cans of gunpowder, three guns ...'

Tom licked his lips as he placed the items on the deck. For people in the bush, guns meant survival. Somers had a heavy hand when either of the boys made a mistake while handling one. He had taught them both how to load cartridges and how to keep them safe and dry. They treated every gun as loaded. Climbing through a fence or over a rock with a loaded gun was out. They took care even when walking on level ground.

If it did go off, the bullet must go into the ground or into the air, not into your mate, or yourself.

Somers continued.

'Twenty bags of flour.' This took time to load. 'Ten pounds of tea ...'

Expensive, thought Matt, *but it was important*. Poor people used a few of the local plants. One coastal bush, called tea-tree, had green leaves that made a good drink.

'One hundred pounds of sugar ...'

'Will that be enough?' asked Tom.

'It'll have to be,' growled Somers. 'Ten pounds of rice, one hundred pounds of salt meat in that barrel.'

'Won't we be catching enough fresh meat, Dad?' said Tom.

'Better safe than sorry. Ten pounds of currants. Good for johnnycakes. Damper tastes better with a few currants. Remember that Matt, since you're the cook. Ten pounds of salt. That will be for on the boat. Plenty of salt on Home Island in a lake. Twenty pounds of soap ...'

The boys groaned. Washing every morning was boring. When Somers left they could at least save on soap!

'Five tins of pepper, four tins of mustard, four tins of curry powder ...'

'Good-oh!' exclaimed Tom. 'I get tired of stew without curry. With Matt cooking we should take ten tins.'

'Fifteen tins of jam,' continued Somers, 'three pint pots, four billies, six knives, forks and spoons ...'

'Why six?' asked Matt.

'Do you think you'll never lose anything? You'll soon get tired of eating with your fingers. Six plates, one camp oven, one frying pan, six dozen boxes of matches. Remember boys, never leave the hut without a box in your pocket. If you get lost you can make a fire and throw on green bushes. The smoke can be seen for miles. Stay near it. Keep the smoke going. Don't keep walking, trying to find the camp like an idiot. You'll be found soon enough if you stay put. Mark the way home if you go looking for anyone lost.

'Yes, Dad,' the boys chorused. They had heard this before, many times.

I'll never get lost, thought Tom scornfully. *Matt will, because he's always dreaming.*

'Twelve blankets. It'll be cold on the island in winter. Fourteen pounds of mixed nails, two hammers and one chisel. Handle the telescope carefully, now. And here're my odds and ends.'

Somers handed over a small bag. 'It's a tin where I throw all my odds and ends. Things I might want some day. Plenty of rope and string. I'll give you all I can spare from the *Silver Gull* when we get to Home Island.' Already they had stopped calling it Middle Island. It was to be their home.

'I can pick up anything extra I need from the farms along the coast when I drop stores but you'll be stuck with what we leave on the island. No shops along the street once we've left Albany. Last of all, pens, ink and paper.'

Tom looked worried. He had no love for school. He left that to Matt.

'Matt, I want you to keep a diary. Fill it in every night after you've had tea. What day it is, what week it is and what month it is. What kind of weather you've been having. I made a measure out of that tin so you can see how much rain falls every day. There's a ruler for mea-

suring. Make a note of what you plant, how many wallabies you catch, how many bags of salt. Anything that's
interesting. Diaries are important. And here are some
books.'

Tom looked disgusted. He was keen to get away from
books.

'The Bible of course,' Dad said. 'Read a bit every
Sunday morning. That should be enough. And here's a
book with all sorts of ideas. The *Bush Boy's Book* it's
called. It tells you how to make traps, rough shelters,
fishing lines. How to make stew, damper and all the
rest over a camp fire. Here's *Robinson Crusoe* and *Coral
Island*, too. Great stories; the first's about a man who
lived for years on an island, the other's about three boys
who were wrecked on a coral island.'

'Didn't Crusoe have a slave called Friday?' asked
Tom. He brightened, 'Matt can be my boy Friday.'

Matt looked glum. He knew the story. Friday didn't
have much of a part except for doing a lot of work.

'Here're some fishing lines. You'll need plenty of
hooks because there'll be lots of fish in the bay. And a
spear.'

The list was long and Matt wondered if the *Silver
Gull* would be able to hold it all. Still, Somers knew
what he was doing.

The livestock came on last. Twenty hens and a
rooster in cages. Later, Somers planned to buy pigs,
sheep, goats and perhaps a cow from farmers along the
coast.

Finally, the goods to sell to the farmers were put on
top of the load, with a number of barrels. Some of these
held water but others contained something Somers
didn't talk about. These he lifted aboard himself.

At last the *Silver Gull* was fully stocked. All they had

to do ashore was finished. All their goodbyes had been said, now the family could leave. There wasn't much room. On the deck was a small boat with oars and sail so the boys could go fishing.

'No more school,' called Tom as he waved to his mates on the wharf, all envious of his luck.

Plenty of time to read, thought Matt.

Somers said nothing, but he also waved. It was good to be off at last.

Then came the anticlimax. The wind blew steadily from the west for most of the year. Perversely it suddenly changed, blowing straight into the harbour entrance. They couldn't move. The boys scrubbed the deck. They spliced rope. They practised knots and they whistled.

'Keep at it,' urged Dad. 'It brings a change of wind and we need it. If I have to stay here another day and listen to those idiots on shore I'll go mad. So whistle!'

At last, in the afternoon, the wind swung to the west. Matt cheerfully obeyed the command to cast off. Their only send-off was a cheer from the few people still lounging on the wharf.

It was a grand day. The wind spun sparkling white caps from wave tops into the troughs. The heavily laden schooner showed her paces as she headed for the entrance of Oyster Harbour. Then they were on the open sea and in the giant swells pushed around the world by the roaring forties.

chapter two

ALBANY TO ESPERANCE

The boys took their turn at the tiller. They learned how to watch the waves, the set of the sails, never to be caught so the ship would turn side-on to be rolled over. When the wind rose to dangerous levels Somers would take the tiller. Even when he was below, asleep in his bunk, he seemed to be listening. He would be up on deck in seconds when the wind changed. Gradually the boys learned to handle the *Silver Gull* even in the worst of weather.

The boys also had time to enjoy the world of the ocean. One bright morning a school of flying fish darted out of the sea near their bow and glided off in terrified flight. Below in the water Matt could see a dark shape as a Spanish mackerel followed in relentless pursuit, intent on its quarry just out of reach. A hundred yards on, each fish dipped into the water, sculling frantically with tail fins to take to the air once more, finally dropping into the sea but turning at right angles to throw off its grim pursuer. In the morning the boys found flying fish lying on the deck — they had collided with the sail during the night. Fried for breakfast they were delicious.

A few days out from Albany, Somers slanted towards the shore, anchoring in a quiet bay. He scanned the shoreline with his telescope, then told the boys they'd work to do to get the barrels ready.

The boys knew the purpose of those barrels. The large one was filled with overproof rum. The smaller ones were for decanting. Matt kept busy boiling water. Somers and Tom used it to bring the fiery spirit to the right strength for sale to the farmers and sealers along the coast. Of all the goods Somers had for sale rum was the most profitable, though illegal.

Every now and again he would scan the shoreline with the telescope, obviously uneasy.

'What are you looking for, Dad?' asked Tom.

'Mind your business, boy,' his father growled. The brothers looked at each other. Why was their father so worried?

Dusk came at last. The ship's lantern swung steadily from the stern.

'Light it, Tom,' ordered Somers.

The boys guessed he was waiting for someone, but who could be living on this desolate stretch of coastline? The long night paled to dawn and no signal came from the dark shore.

'Who are you waiting for, Dad?' asked Matt, at last.

'Michael. The last of the Fenians. You know, the Irish rebels. I had a mob of them under me in the convict ship. We were warned how dangerous rebels could be. I dunno. Brave men they were. It's every man's right to fight for freedom. Still they broke the law.'

Somers sipped at a mug of rum. 'Well spoken, they were though.'

The boys kept silent, hardly breathing. This was adventure. Their father had never told them of his early days in England or of life on the convict ship. They glanced at each other. Perhaps Dad was changing or perhaps it was only the rum! Tom refilled his father's mug. He hardly seemed to notice, except to take another drink.

'I'll never forget that trip in the *Bella*. Good ship she was. A good captain and a good surgeon. That's what you need. Strong men in command and you have a safe ship.'

'At school we were told how dangerous the Fenians were,' volunteered Tom.

'Teachers ...' jeered Somers. 'What do they know of real life? The Fenians wanted to be free of the old country. Run their own affairs. I dunno, sometimes when I look at this new land perhaps they were right. Perhaps we should be free of old England too. Anyhow they were useful on board. Helped save us during a storm when our own sailors were too scared to go aloft.

'And make you laugh! The stories they told. They brought out their own newspaper too. Called it the *Wild Goose*.'

'Silly name,' muttered Tom.

'Listen and learn,' his father spoke sternly. 'When Protestant William became King of England, a lot of the Irish gentry fled to France with the old King James and his son, Charles, papists we English kicked out. These Irish called him the 'king over the water.' They formed a regiment which they named The Wild Geese. They hoped to come back home just like the wild geese which flew back to Ireland each spring to nest on their homeland.

'But not a word to anyone. It would be the end of me if the police knew I was helping a Fenian to escape. *And* of you boys. The orphanage for you if I'm caught.'

For a week they waited. All the rum casks had been filled. They spent the time fishing, talking and watching. At last Somers gave the order to up anchor and away.

'Good luck to him,' he muttered as they headed out to sea.

After supper that night, everything cleared away, Matt stood at the stern. He thought of Michael and The Wild Geese while fish jumped in glittering showers around the boat. He looked towards the eastern horizon. An island lay out there. One day it would be theirs.

Finally they reached Esperance, the last port in the State. There was an unpleasant surprise waiting.

'Look Dad. There's a policeman!'

Somers greeted the officer jovially. The Fenian had not been waiting. He was not worried. The rum was very carefully stowed. The man jumped on board to search the ship. It did not take long.

'All okay, Captain. Sorry about that. Another busybody wasting my time.'

He jumped off, waved and was gone.

'Right boys. Let's unload the stores for Esperance, then get going. Don't want to waste the wind.'

A few hours later they were headed for Home Island.

chapter three

THE LAST LEG

The *Silver Gull* raced along in the strong westerlies. At times the gigantic surges were frightening.

'The size of the wave doesn't matter,' said Somers. 'So long as each crest is far enough apart the *Gull* will lift. Then she will wait for the next wave. Not to worry, Matt, you'll soon get the hang of it. Keep your mind on the sea, not on those birds flying over your head.' Even so Somers loved the birds flying free. They seemed to fit in with his new mood.

'That wandering albatross is a wonderful flier. Some landlubbers think the birds are sacred because they carry the souls of sailors who died at sea. Y'know there's a poem about a sailor who killed an albatross and had bad luck.'

'Yes,' said Matt eagerly, glad that Tom was asleep below. '"The Ancient Mariner" it's called, and this man had to wander the world forever, telling people of the evil deed he had done.' He began to recite:

God save thee, Ancient Mariner;
From the fiends that plague thee thus!
Why look'st thou so? – With my crossbow
I shot the albatross.

'Well Matt, not to worry. I don't have a crossbow and
the guns are safe in the cabin. But it wasn't like that on
the *Bella*. We used to bait a line with salt pork – that's
about all we had to eat towards the end – and when an
albatross landed on the water to swallow the meat we'd
haul it on board – fresh meat was rare and we all
hankered for it. Not that we wasted the rest of each
bird. Webs on the feet we made into purses and tobacco
pouches. Hollow leg bones we used as stems for our
pipes. Even turned the feathers into warm rugs.'

The days passed as Somers told stories of his early
days and his hopes of a golden future. Tom dreamt of
plans for a Somers Line, a fleet of small ships to take
over the coastal trade, just in the west, then moving to
the eastern colonies, with father and sons making a
powerful group. There was talk of a telegraph line to
run along the coastline linking east and west. That
would mean more business servicing the telegraph
stations' staff.

Every few days the *Silver Gull* headed for the shore.
Safely anchored in a sheltered bay, or protected by
offshore sandbanks, Somers rowed ashore to meet his
customers.

There were no jetties along the coast. They landed all
the stores on the beach. Sometimes they saw a large
store box placed on the dune with a list of needs inside.
More often they found a farmer and his family camped

on the beach for a holiday of fishing and swimming until the *Silver Gull* arrived. There was plenty of fishing. King George whiting was the best, grilled over hot coals.

'A fish fit for King George himself,' said Somers, although he knew that George was long dead and his daughter Victoria was queen.

Once they saw a giant shoal of salmon move in close to the shore. The fish sheltered all day behind a reef and they noticed a clear space with a giant fish in the centre of the school.

'What's that?' asked Matt, turning to his father.

'A white shark. Most dangerous animal in the sea. Can grow twenty feet long and could bite you in half if he caught you. I've seen a shark kill a big sea lion with one bite. These fish know enough to give the shark a clear space. If it heads towards them, they swim just a bit faster, always keeping their distance.'

'What's it waiting for then?' Tom asked. 'If it can't catch any fish you'd think it would get tired of that and look somewhere else.'

'Ah,' said Somers. 'In every big mob of animals, and that school of salmon would probably weigh about a thousand tons, with tens of thousands of fish ...'

'Wow,' gasped Tom. 'Why don't we become fishermen, Dad? With a thousand tons of fish we could make our fortunes.'

Somers pondered this new idea. Perhaps the boy was right. Fish could be dried in the sun or smoked over fires.

'Well Tom, you may have something there. Some call the white shark the white death, because it's feared so much among the sealers and whalers. In that school of salmon there would be among the thousands of healthy fish a few sick ones. Perhaps with a torn fin or a gash from a reef. As the shark moves slowly through the school it sees the one that's a bit slower than its mates. That's the one the hunter picks and makes a dash. The sick animal is just a bit slower and the hunter has its meal.'

Sometimes they managed to shoot a wallaby and then had fresh meat. There were black duck and grey teal in coastal lagoons. On the rocks were oysters in their thousands.

Occasionally they picked up a passenger for a station further along the coast.

Somers promised the boys they could come with him on one of his return voyages, when he came inshore to pick up bales of wool to be sold in Albany.

'Have to get to know your customers,' he explained. 'The station staff all come down with the wool for a beach holiday. They bring it in wagons. Mostly they use horses but some are using camels now. If the going's rough they load the wool onto the camels. I sell their wool in Albany, take out what money they owe me for stores and cartage, and put the rest into the bank for them.'

'They trust you with all their money?' asked Tom in amazement.

'A man wouldn't last long in the bush if he cheated.'

'Would you tell the police?' asked Matt.

'Not out here. We make our own law. Our own punishments too.' He would say no more. His mouth shut in the look that had earned him the reputation of being a hard man, and not one to be crossed.

It had been a good run and at the last stop before Home Island, Somers was out of all the trade stores.

It'll be a good life, he thought. *I'll only need one big run a year. Out from Albany to sell stores, back again to pick up wool, and the rest of the time on Home Island. With wallaby skins and salt we might make an extra run to port. Could get seal skins if we're lucky.*

'How long before we reach Home Island, Dad?' asked Tom, the next day.

'H'mm. Good following wind. Maybe four hours with luck ...'

A few silver gulls stayed with their namesake. Matthew tossed them the remains of some damper saying, 'Since we're the *Silver Gull* we'd better give them something. Might bring us luck. Why did you choose the name, Dad?'

Somers thought for a time. 'They're good clean birds, good movers in all kinds of weather. They travel along shorelines just like us and they pick up anything they want, just like us.'

Further out to sea the gulls left them for the mainland. They were shorebirds, landlubbers compared to the stately albatross.

'Up that mast boy, now, and look for land.'

Before Matt could move Tom had shinned up and looked to the east. He gave a shout, 'Land ho! There it is.'

chapter four

HOME ISLAND

omers and Matt were on their feet staring. Sure enough there was a grey blur on the horizon. As the minutes passed they saw a peak rising out of the sea. Gradually it became part of a mountain on the western half of an island. They sailed along the north shoreline into calmer water. Forest-clad slopes led into green valleys with, high above, a rock-tipped peak.

'Bald Mountain,' cried Tom. 'I name it Bald Mountain!'

Then came a point, and behind it a glorious bay with a sandy beach. This would be their harbour, and somewhere along that shore would be their new home.

'Home Bay,' said Somers quietly, 'and Home Beach. We'll call that creek running into Home Bay after Ann. Just there looks to be the place to build our hut.'

They were all silent — the boys thought how much their mother would have loved this place. They could see a granite headland backed by deep green moonah trees in the distance. On the rocks a colony of birds stared at the boat but showed no alarm. A few flew off. They could see it was a rookery with some birds sitting on nests and some feeding chicks.

'I know what they are,' shouted Matt. 'Black-faced shags. I name this place Shag Point,' he cried in triumph.

Somers approved. 'We'll make a map of Home Island and you can both give names to places we need to visit often.'

Tom looked around, trying to find something more he could name, but he decided to wait until they had anchored and gone ashore. He dreamed of some important place being named after him.

Somers ran the boat close in, then anchored in clear water with a sandy bottom where the hook gripped firmly.

'She'll hold,' he said with satisfaction. 'Good holding ground even in a strong wind.'

'Let's go ashore,' cried the boys.

Somers agreed, 'I'll get the dinghy into the water.'

The boys did not wait for any slow boat. It was a warm day and they leapt overboard. Both swam like fish. Swimming was the main summer sport in Albany. Tom was a very powerful swimmer and had won all his school races.

'Home Island, Home Island,' shouted Matt and danced a jig on the beach in excitement. Then he turned half-a-dozen perfect cartwheels along the sand before running after Tom who had already begun to move towards the sand-dunes. The beach stretched for about two miles in a perfect half-moon.

Behind the dunes the grey-green of wattles was backed by the dense green of moonah trees. The creek was lined with paperbarks and some ducks paddled quietly upstream. Here was the family's freshwater supply.

Somers was now ashore and called to the boys to help him haul the dinghy above high watermark. Then he took the small dinghy anchor even higher and dug it into the sand. The boys watched and learned.

'Better safe than sorry,' was Somers' motto. He had drummed into them to always make sure the boat was safe before doing anything else.

Somers stood to survey their new kingdom. To the west the low-lying plain led to forests of tall trees that promised good soil. He could see a deep valley that could shelter many wallabies. High above towered the granite peak, huge boulders had tumbled down its slopes. Bald Mountain is a good name, he thought.

He turned to the boys. 'Work first. We'll explore tomorrow.'

They jumped to this command. By late afternoon all the most needed stores were ashore. A rough shelter of brushwood and canvas was up, in case of night showers.

'Always a chance of heavy dew on clear nights,' explained Somers, 'especially if the wind drops.'

Soon they had a camp fire alight and the family had settled to a meal of stew. Salt pork and potatoes were filling, even if boring.

'We'll have fresh meat tomorrow,' Somers promised. 'Tonight is hard tack with damper. And because it's our first night, we'll ...'

He ran a little rum and water into three mugs and they all stood and drank to their future on Home Island.

The boys slept soundly, curled up on some bags.

The ringing dawn chorus of bush birds woke Matt. The fire was going, and breakfast was ready. In the pot a stew bubbled.

Matt stared in surprise. 'What do you have cooking there, Dad?'

His father grunted. 'While you were fast asleep and burning daylight, I was up and fishing. Caught breakfast for you. Now up you get and have a wash. We're going exploring.'

What a day for it! The sun was shining brightly. Overhead a wedge-tailed eagle and a white-breasted sea eagle patrolled the skies. Far out to sea fairy penguins gave their barking call as they searched for fish. In the bay a line of dolphins broke the surface, sending water drops shining like diamonds in the early morning light.

'Let's climb the mountain first,' urged Tom.

'Good idea, son. We can see the shape of our new home from up there. Give me a chance to make a rough map. Bring your notebook and pencil, Matt. Let's get moving. We've a lot to see today.'

Though only fifteen hundred feet high, the mountain dominated the island. Down one slope, smooth rock ran gently to the sea and this made for easy climbing. Once on the summit they could see the majestic rollers moving from the west, to smash like battering rams against the coast, sending up a continuous shower of spray. Even though there was little wind in sheltered Home Bay, the roaring forties pushed mountains of water to hammer against anything which stood in the path of the waves. Somers was grateful they had such a good harbour on the north side.

From this high point they could see that the eastern side of the island was not granite but a mixture of sand and limestone rocks. At one place the sand-dunes encircled an almost circular lake that glowed pink in the morning sun.

'Pink Lake,' said Tom in a matter-of-fact tone. Matt

thought this was too commonplace for such a beautiful piece of water which lay like a great eye staring at the heavens.

'Pink Lake it is,' agreed Somers as he added the name to the sketch he was making. Soon he had all the important features mapped. They could see three sandy beaches. The largest was Home Beach, where they had built the rough shelter the day before. Then there was an eastern beach, which was smaller but could provide another site for a hut, and to the south was a small patch of sand, poorly protected from the giant rollers.

'We'll head to the south side first,' declared Somers. 'There's a small peak there.'

'Tom's Peak?' the older boy asked.

'All right,' agreed Somers. 'Tom's Peak it will be. Now get going.'

Two hours later, tired and scratched, they reached the beach. It had been a hard slog, not only because of the thick shrubbery but also because of a great tangle of dodder laurel climbing over the bushes. All were glad when they broke out of this green jungle and reached the shore. The beach was made entirely of empty shells that tinkled as they walked over them.

'Stop!' Somers held up his hand. 'Seals! What a piece of luck. Fur seals too. Those will bring good prices in Albany.'

Matt gazed at the beautiful creatures stretched out on the beach. A baby nuzzled up to its mother and began drinking milk from her teat. At another place a larger seal reared up to look at the intruders. He was a bull seal, the master of this harem, ready to defend the females against any enemy. How could people kill such lovely creatures, Matt thought. But he didn't say a word.

He knew what Somers would say and what Tom would say. Indeed what every other person in Albany would say.

'Will we be hunting them, Dad?' Tom asked eagerly.

'No,' said Somers. 'Not 'til I come back. Seals can be dangerous. Don't get too near. One bite from a seal and you could be badly injured, even killed. Come on, Matt. Forget about those shells. You'll find plenty on Home Beach and you can come back for more later.'

Somers nodded with satisfaction when they reached the eastern beach. 'This will be a good spot to load the skins. Not a bad harbour, but I think Home Beach is better.'

'The sand is singing,' cried Matt. 'Listen!' He scuffed his feet over the beach. They all did the same, listening to what sounded like music.

'Come on. Let's have a look at the lake.'

'Pink Lake,' reminded Tom.

It was only a ten-minute walk over the dunes and the boys were surprised to find the water looked clear, not pink. Towards the far edge it gradually shaded to a rosy flush. Somers was interested in the thick rim of salt along the edge.

'It will be easy to carry the bags to the beach,' he explained. 'All you'll have to do is bag the salt clear of the edge. We can knock up a wheelbarrow to carry the bags. This salt will make us plenty of money among the sealers and settlers. Everyone wants salt.' The boys didn't look so happy. Bagging salt in the hot sun didn't seem much fun.

'Come on,' said their father, 'let's head for Home Beach. We have a lot to do before I leave you.'

It was nice to be back home and have a quick lunch.

The first job was to make a safe shelter for the hens that had been cooped up for so long. Somers had brought a roll of netting to make a yard. They made the run under some shrubby tea-trees where the fowls would be sheltered from both hot sun and strong winds.

'Why can't we just let them run free?' asked Matt.

'They would soon go wild and you'd never catch them again. This island is too big. And just look up in the sky, lad. You'll see another reason.'

High overhead two huge brown birds with wedge-shaped tails were circling, watching what was happening. Curious and unafraid they came lower.

'Those eagles will be the end of our hens. Get me the gun, Tom,' said Somers.

Tom raced off and returned with the gun, pleading, 'Let me, Dad?'

'You'll have plenty of shooting later,' Somers said as he aimed and fired.

A bunch of feathers sprang from one bird, and both flew fast away from the beach. Somers looked disappointed. He was proud of his shooting but birds in flight were not easy targets. Matt was secretly pleased.

'Well,' said Somers, 'we're going to need a roof on that fowl run otherwise we'll lose the lot. You boys won't always be here to scare off those eagles. Clever brutes. They'll wait 'til they see you walking away from the hut, then swoop. Get some wattle sticks, Matt, and we'll soon have a roof. We shouldn't waste ammunition shooting at birds. Keep it for more important targets. Scare them away every now and again with a shot or two. Don't look so glum, Matt. I know you hate to see birds killed but if you want eggs for breakfast then it's either them or you. Make up your mind.'

Matt decided he'd try and make a scarecrow like

those on the farms near Albany. If the birds saw something that looked like a person near the hut they might keep away.

'Now for a well,' Somers decided. He found a seepage about fifty yards from the hut, sheltered among the trees, and began digging in the soft soil.

'Why not just get water from the creek or dig a well near the hut?' asked Tom.

'Good, clean water is important. A well in sand is always clean, that's one thing I've learned. And pure. No muck from animals. The hut is too near the sea.'

Water seeped into the well a few feet down but Somers kept on digging so even in the height of summer there would be plenty. He lined the sides with short poles so sand would not fall in.

'There you are boys. Fresh water for the whole year. Later, when we build a proper house, I'll make a deep well and might even put in a windmill so we can pump water to the house. This will do for the next few months until I get back. Now for the hut. We'll cut a good supply of wattle.'

He thought back to the sheds he had built in England, making the walls and roofs out of supple sticks. Once the ends were firmly in the ground, twisting a kind of lattice was the next step. Sometimes he had made the mesh and then dug one end into the ground. They used to slap mud on to make a snug shelter of wattle and daub.

Around Albany the local acacia gave the best sticks, so gradually the small tree was called wattle. It was a pretty plant. In the middle of winter beautiful balls of yellow flowers blossomed, changing grey landscapes to golden.

Somers described what he wanted. 'It doesn't have to

be all wattle sticks. Any tree that has stems or branches about nine feet long and as thick as my thumb will do. It must be supple. Wattle is best but I can use gum trees, spearwood, paperbarks, tea-trees. They must be supple so we can twist them around each other. Get the idea?'

Matt asked, 'Is spearwood what the Aborigines use to make spears?'

'Yes, and I've seen some on the island.'

'How many sticks do you want?' asked Tom, ever practical.

'Plenty,' replied Somers. 'Any left over we can use for cupboards, shelves, lots of things. Let's go.'

The next morning a good pile of sticks lay ready, but the first job was to bring limestone boulders for the fireplace. The family worked hard. The boys turned to gathering mud from the creek. Somers placed the fireplace stones together, carefully selecting those that fitted neatly and stood free. They plastered the stones with mud to help hold the fireplace firm. Next it was time to build the walls of the hut, making sure the fireplace was on the outside. No chance then of the fire setting the wattle and daub walls alight.

Gradually the mesh of intertwined wattle sticks stretched out to reach the larger timber poles that made the corners of the hut. A simple box about twenty feet by twenty feet was soon standing. Then came the daubing with mud, followed by a roof of wattle sticks to keep out the rain. More mud was needed to bind this. Last of all their father had the boys gather tea-tree branches to cover the whole roof with a layer of brush to make a thatch, with an overhang to protect the walls from rain. The job was finished before dark.

'Let's hunt up a white ant mound,' said Somers next

morning. 'I saw one back in the bush.'

They gathered around a grey-looking mound. Dad broke it open with his axe. Thousands of greyish-white insects poured out in frantic anger, trying to defend their home.

'White ants,' said Somers.

'They don't look like ants,' objected Matt. 'Much too soft. I wonder if these are what that Yankee from the whaler called termites? He said we had to watch out or they would eat our houses.'

'Who cares?' said Tom. 'What use are they, Dad?'

'You'll soon see, lad. On the mainland we used clay and cow dung but no cows here. White ant nests are even better for making floors. Fill those bags and we'll get these lumps back to the hut.'

Somers broke up three insect mounds before he was satisfied. All the big lumps were smashed into smaller ones on the hut floor. Then the boys brought water and softened this hard material to grey mud. They smoothed the mud with a plank until it covered the floor. The last stretch was the bit near the door so they could walk outside.

'Right,' said Somers with relief, 'we've been working hard. Let's go fishing.'

At Home Beach the boys stripped and dived in. Feeling fresh and frisky from the cool water, they raced along the beach until they were dry enough to put their clothes on. They found some ruins of old huts. Their father told them the place used to be a whalers' camp and that he had heard stories that treasure was buried there.

On the rocks they gathered pieces of limpet for bait, and spread along the sand, holding their fishing lines.

Tom dug a hole in the beach and found a white crab that made good bait. The boys watched these ghost crabs running like wraiths, almost invisible on the sand. At dusk, ghost crabs came out in hundreds, looking for food scraps along the dunes. Matt picked one up to keep as a pet. *I'll feed it on scraps*, he thought.

They caught plenty of fish, enough for tea, and for breakfast the next day.

Back at the hut they found that the heat from the sun and the dry wind had baked the floor hard.

'That will last a lifetime,' said Somers with satisfaction. 'They make tennis courts out of white ant mounds. Almost as good as cement. Now to knock up some furniture for you boys. And beds for all of us.'

'What will we use?' wondered Matt.

'No problem. There's plenty of timber. With an axe any good bushman can make all he needs. Cut some poles. Four short ones for each bed as bedposts. Cross posts for the ends, and two long ones, longer than any of us. Thread these through the big bags we brought for carrying our stores. That will make the bed. You can fill other bags with grass to make a mattress. Or, if you like, get branches of gum leaves. I've used those in the bush. Change the leaves every few weeks. Then you'll have the smell of eucalypt leaves every night. It will stop you from getting colds. Ann always swore by eucalyptus oil to keep off colds. With our blankets you'll be as snug as bugs in rugs.'

Somers worked with hammer and axe to make cupboards and shelves for the telescope and tools he was leaving with the boys. At night they sat around the fireplace, listening to the kettle singing as it hung from an iron hook just above the flames. The oil lamp and the light from the fire gave some light, although not enough for reading so Matt could only sit and dream. It was a great place, perfect for dreaming!

Tom looked around the hut and wondered at all the things Somers had made with pieces of strong wire, an axe, hammer and nails. He hoped he could grow to be as good at everything as Somers. And as tough too. Nobody bullied Somers. Nobody would ever bully him.

And he'd look after Matt while Somers was away.

Somers also looked around the hut and at his two sons. He had thought his world had ended when Ann died. But life could be good. Perhaps the Somers' luck had changed.

A week later a storm of rain and wind tested the roof and walls. Somers was satisfied, 'It'll do until I get back.'

The next day, after a breakfast of fresh eggs and fish, Somers had a last talk with his sons before he left on the long voyage to Albany, and the hard work of getting the wool from the farmers along the coast on board the *Silver Gull*. Luckily the wind had backed to the east so he would have a good run.

'Now,' he said, 'you know what you have to do. Every morning I want Tom to mark off the day on the calendar. Matt, every night before you go to bed you'll make an entry into the log about what kind of weather you had, tide, sun and phase of moon. What work you did. How many wallabies you trapped. How many bags of salt you stacked. Make a note of how much rain fell in that tin I put on the post near the hut. Make as many notes as you can. Better for your log to have too much than too little.'

Matt nodded. He was keen on writing. Keeping a diary, or log as Somers called it, would be fun, not work.

Somers turned to Tom. 'Now for the salt. Gather it when the weather's good and stack it in heaps. You know just how I want it. I'll expect to see a good pile of bags when I get back. Sew the bags on wet days. I'm taking a sample to Albany to make sure it's the kind everyone wants. Now, anything else?'

'Skins,' said Tom promptly.

'Of course. Set the snares each afternoon to catch the wallabies as they come out to feed during the night. You know where the runs are. Don't forget early every morning go to every snare. If any wallaby is still alive, kill it the way I showed you. Take each body back to the camp, skin it and use the meat for food. Matt will turn it into good stews. The skins you will peg out and rub with salt. As soon as they're dry, roll each into a bundle and store them in that small shed I made on the side of the hut. Keep them out of the rain otherwise they'll rot.

'Saturdays you mend your clothes, do any work on the hut. Don't set any snares Saturday. That leaves Sunday free. On Sunday morning, Matt, you read something from the Bible. Then you can do what you like. Take the dinghy and sail over to Goose Island but no further. Too dangerous. Explore the mountain and the bush. Keep your eyes open for anything worthwhile. Collect any good timber that washes ashore.'

Tom stood up. He was confident they could carry out all those instructions. He was keen to start.

'Well, if you can't look after yourself I've failed,' ended Somers. 'At your age Tom, I was a carpenter and earning a good wage. You know the rules about guns. I don't want any accidents. Tom, you'll be in charge of the guns and powder.'

They are good boys, he thought. *Matthew takes after Ann. A bit soft in his ways but bright. Quick as a flash and that's what Tom needs. Somebody he can look after but bright enough to be useful. Tom is a chip off the old block. Reminds me of my Dad. Solid as oak. The boys'll be better off here than in Albany. No way of getting into trouble.*

'Right boys. It's off to the ship. You can have the day off when I've gone.'

Somers never gave much outward show of affection. *To hug him would be like hugging a jarrah tree*, thought Matt. *Just as rough and just as hard.*

The boys were quiet as they watched the *Silver Gull* move from the bay at a spanking pace. The east wind filled the sails as she disappeared around the headland to the west.

Home Island's mine now, thought Tom proudly, *and Matt had better know who's boss. I'm in Dad's shoes.*

'An island all of our own,' cried Matt and turned a cartwheel in glee. 'It's like Robinson Crusoe. You can be Crusoe and I'll be Man Friday.'

'You're the wrong colour,' retorted Tom. 'And you're not a man yet.'

Matt had already run ahead. 'I'm going fishing, Tom. Coming? Come on Spot!' he shouted.

The two boys ran off along the beach, Spot wagging his tail enthusiastically. What dog could ask for more?

And what more could boys ask for?

chapter five

CRUSOE BOYS

Matt and Tom began a new life as rulers of a small island with a large population! This included seabirds and wallabies. These small marsupials hopped stealthily through the scrub along well-defined trails. They fed after dark, safe from wedge-tailed eagles and from sea eagles — those alert sky hunters large enough to lift a tammar from the ground and carry it away to devour at leisure in the treetops or on a convenient rock.

At night the boys often heard a tammar make a thumping noise. They guessed the wallaby was bringing its hind feet down hard on the ground, as a warning to its friends nearby.

At dusk Matt and Tom went out with their wire snares, carefully setting them along the main wallaby trails which had been used by the animals for generation after generation. The unsuspecting tammars pushed their heads through the snares as they searched for grass and fungi. Once trapped they struggled frantically. A few minutes later they were dead, strangled by the noose. Matt wished there was a less cruel way of killing them but he kept quiet about it. He knew Tom would laugh at him.

Soon after dawn the boys went back along their line of traps to bring the limp bodies back to the hut. Both worked fast to skin their victims. Matt selected the meat he wanted for meals. With the pieces, plus potatoes and onions, he made stew. This was their regular standby.

He used to throw unwanted meat scraps into the water near where they went fishing until one day a huge fin broke the water's surface. A vast, greyish-white hulk moved among the scraps of floating meat, snapping them up in lazy fashion. Each time the huge jaw opened the boys could see lines of razor-sharp triangular teeth.

'It's the great white shark,' breathed Tom, too scared even to speak loudly. 'The white death!'

When they caught a whiting or flathead, a tommy rough or a small salmon, they gutted it, then threw the fish on the coals. After a few minutes they turned it over. When they lifted it onto a plate the skin and scales came off in one piece. They had learned this trick from the Aboriginal boys and girls around Albany. Their friends laughed when they cleaned out the internal organs.

'Leave them,' they scoffed, 'makes it taste better.'

Somers had said, 'I don't like innards.' The boys followed his example. Matt tried many experiments with his cooking, not always with good results.

'What's this?' Tom would growl in disgust. 'Here Spot.

You try it but don't blame me if you get poisoned.' Spot had learned to be careful and would sniff at Matt's latest experiment before devouring it. Matt liked the dog's attitude better than Tom's.

One day Matt decided to try something new. Before the wallaby was skinned he took it down to the creek where he gutted it. He washed the inside clean in the water, stuffed it with damper and onions, then sewed the slit tight. With mud from the creekbed he plastered the body until it became a round shape, with the head and back legs sticking out.

Tom strolled over to watch.

'What are you going to do with those bits?'

'They'll get burned off in the coals. I know it looks funny but let's give it a go.'

The boys went back to the camp and made a fire well away from the hut. The gum tree branches and other scraps burned to coals. With a spade Matt made a small hollow nearby and shovelled in the coals. Then he lowered the wallaby in and heaped more hot coals over the ball of mud until it disappeared into the heart of the glowing heap.

'There,' he said with satisfaction, 'tonight that'll be a great meal.'

'You're leaving it to cook all day?' asked Tom in amazement.

'I think that's what Dad said.'

'Ah, well. We can always fall back on the stew,' his brother suggested. Then looked thoughtfully at the heap of coals with smoke spiralling lazily upwards.

'Gypsies cook hedgehogs that way. We could try one of those spiny anteaters.'

'Yes. Let's try lots of things. When Dad comes back

we'll choose the best and have a great feast!'

In the late afternoon Matt scraped away the ash and, with the spade, lifted out the blackened ball. It was very hot so he was careful, using a hammer to break open the hardened clay. The wallaby fur was only singed and when it was cool enough he stripped it all away. The meat was beautifully cooked.

'A meal fit for a king,' crowed Matt, after they had finished eating.

Tom grunted approval. Baked food was delicious.

After this they wrapped all kinds of animals in mud for cooking. When they were lucky enough to catch ducks in traps they cooked them with the feathers still in place. They even cooked a goanna they ran down after it had come to raid their fowl yard. Matt became bolder and tried different stuffings, instead of just damper and onion.

But life was not all hunting tammars or going fishing. Deep in the forest was the garden, in a patch open to the sky. The sun poured in long enough to keep plants growing, and the trees provided shelter from the strong winds.

Tom decided he was the farmer as Matt was doing the cooking. He planted potatoes, onions, broad beans, garden peas, lettuce, radishes and some other seeds which had lost their labels, but he hoped for the best. Somers had warned them about how important it was to eat their greens.

'If you don't you'll get scurvy. Barcoo rot they call it out here. It's just plain old scurvy which killed more seamen than cannonballs.'

'What do the Aborigines do?' asked Matt, curious about how they survived, as they grew no plants but just wandered through the bush catching animals, or went fishing, gathering sea creatures in the shallow water.

Somers had taken them for a walk instead of answering. He stopped at a blackboy and broke off the stiff green stems to show the white bases. These were soft and tasty. Near the beach they found shrubs covered with golden berries, like small grapes. These were soft and sweet. The boys wanted to chew the rich red fruits of the zamia which looked like huge pineapples but Somers warned them these needed treatment. Raw they could be poisonous. He hadn't yet learned how to treat them to get rid of the poison. Aboriginal people knew what to do but the treatment was complicated.

Near the shore Somers had showed them what he called New Zealand spinach which could be eaten raw. They agreed it was almost as good as lettuce and said they would eat it regularly. In the sea, growing on the rocks, was a green seaweed Somers called sea lettuce. This too, though a bit tough, tasted good enough to add to their greens.

Somers had then told them the Aborigines ate far more plant than animal food. The women gathered seeds, berries and fruits. Without the women's work the tribe would starve.

Tom was sure his garden would supply all they needed without any bush greens. Every day he checked his plants. The vegetables were all growing well.

One day he came running back from the garden in the forest roaring with anger.

'The bloody things. I'll murder them.'

'What's up?' cried Matt in alarm.

Tom was shaking his fist towards the garden. 'Come and see what they've done!'

They ran to the garden. All the shoots which had made the garden look so good were gone, grazed flat to the ground.

'Those wallabies,' shouted Tom, 'came in last night and ate them all. I'll kill them.'

Matt didn't think it tactful to point out they had both been killing tammars for some time! Tom sat on a tree stump and stared at his ruined plants.

'We need a fence,' suggested Matt.

'Of course we'll need a bloody fence, stupid. But what about my garden? Weeks of growing all gone.' He fell silent thinking about what needed to be done. Then his face brightened.

'I wonder ... remember that farm at Albany where we went to look at the wheat? The farmer had let his sheep in there to graze on the young shoots. He said a bit of pruning made the wheat grow faster. Perhaps not all my plants are ruined. Come on, Matt. Let's cut wattle sticks for a fence.'

Hours later the fence was ready with wattle sticks driven into the ground to enclose the garden. It was low enough for the boys to climb over, but too high for wallabies to jump. Or at least they hoped so.

'Just like Robinson Crusoe,' said Matt proudly. 'Remember how he built a fence to keep in the goats? I hope the wallabies can't jump it.'

'If they jump in they won't ever jump out again,' promised Tom with a scowl.

The wallabies never attacked the garden again.

Gardening, fishing and cooking were all fun. But when the weather was fine the boys gathered salt from Pink Lake. They hated the job, but Somers' orders kept them working hard. They carried the loads on shovels to the shore and dumped them in a heap above the high water level. As each pile grew large enough they covered it with branches. When the leaves were dry they set them alight. The heat of the fire melted the surface salt. This formed a crust about six inches thick, hard enough to stop the rain dissolving the heap, and making a kind of salt roof. Sometimes it rained before they could start the fire. Then they had to watch helplessly as the water turned their salt hillocks into a muddy mess.

Cuts festered when they worked in the salty water so they had to stop working until the wounds healed. Their father had warned them never to neglect a cut. In the hut they had some goanna salve to plaster over any wound.

They often dropped things into the shallow lake water. Matt threw in a green branch and, after a few weeks, dragged it out covered with a thick layer of salt. It looked quite beautiful so he took it home to add to his treasures.

Usually Matt's salt branch was dry but one day he noticed it had become quite damp. A few hours later clouds piled up on the western horizon and that night it rained hard. The same thing happened a week later and Matt realised he had made a kind of barometer. When his salty leaves became damp it meant rain; when dry, fine weather. This helped them to decide when to start burning the branches on the salt piles since it gave them a few hours' warning of rain.

The boys waged constant war against the goannas which raided the fowl yard. They found the smallest hole and pushed their long, slim bodies through. When cornered a goanna would rear high in the air on its large back legs and make a dash at Matt or Tom, hissing loudly and slipping its long forked tongue in and out. The boys soon learned this was mainly bluff, though once Tom got bitten on his leg, which took a long while to heal. Usually the goannas raced up a tree trunk out of harm's way.

Once when Tom was chasing a lizard on a bare patch of ground it saw Matt standing still. Mistaking him for a small tree it raced up his body. The sharp claws scratched all the way as it went to the top of his head. It stared wildly around, looking for a taller tree. While Matt screeched in a mixture of pain and terror, Tom laughed and laughed so much that the goanna made its escape.

On another occasion, Tom found a dead goanna and threw it into Pink Lake. Some weeks later he removed the salty body and spread it in a natural looking way on a rock. The boys hid behind a bush and waited until the wedge-tailed eagle, which was always soaring high in the air, swooped to clutch the goanna in its sharp talons. It did look a bit puzzled as it peered at the goanna as though wondering why it was not struggling. The bird kept flying until it reached a tall tree where it began to devour its tasty looking victim.

'I wonder how it will like the taste of that?' said Tom, who had no liking for the eagles which ate his hens.

'Very thirsty after a salted goanna,' said Matt who had a fondness for eagles and wished he could soar in the air.

There was plenty of time for wandering along the beach to see what had been washed up. Tom always walked slightly ahead of Matt so he could have first claim on anything they found. Matt had to be content with things his older brother did not want. They climbed over some limestone rocks and Tom rushed forward.

'Wow,' he cried. 'Just look at that!'

Wedged in the rocks was a box with a bony spear sticking out of one side. It had pierced the thick wood. Almost an arm's length of spear was held firm but the boys could see that while the pointed end was still sharp and undamaged the broader part had broken away.

'It's a sword from a swordfish! Remember that one the fishermen caught in Albany. Must have weighed a ton and it had a sword just like this.'

Tom tried to pull out the sword but it had wedged too firmly.

'I'll chop it out later,' he said as he lifted the box to carry this treasure back to the hut.

'Why not keep it just as it is? I bet nobody else would have anything like this. There are plenty of swords taken from fish which have been caught but nothing as unusual as this. The fish could have charged the box thinking it was an enemy. And then had to shake its head to try to get rid of the box, but its sword broke off.'

'I wonder how the fish is getting on with no sword?' Tom commented. 'Still I s'pose it could still catch food even with a broken sword.'

'Can I have this for my museum?' asked Matt hopefully.

'No fear,' replied Tom. 'Finders keepers, losers weepers. Just think what the kids in Albany will say when I show them this,' he finished triumphantly. Which was just what Matt had been thinking!

Then Matt found his treasure. At first it didn't look too promising. Just a big black ball of feathers out of which stuck a powerful beak and two webbed feet.

'Is it alive?' asked Tom.

Matt poked at the bird and the beak slashed out. He yelped.

'The brute. Just look. It's drawn blood.'

'Let me get at it,' volunteered Tom. 'I'll soon kill it.'

'No,' cried Matt. 'It's mine. You found the sword. I found the bird. It's mine.'

'You can have it for what good it will be. It must be sick and it'll soon die.'

'The poor bird's frightened. I know what it is. It's a penguin but it's bigger than the fairy penguins we have around here.'

'Pretty funny looking penguin. It looks nice and fat. I wonder if it would be good to eat.'

Tom's animal world was divided into the kinds you could eat, the kinds you had to be careful about, and the rest.

'We've plenty of food,' protested Matt. 'Still I wonder why it's so fat? Ah well, so long as it eats fish I can keep it well fed and then we'll see what happens.'

'I wonder what Spot will think of your new pet? And where is Spot?'

Just then the dog came galloping up. It stopped with a crash when it saw the penguin. Cautiously it approached and sniffed, ready to believe what its nose told it rather than its eyes.

Home Island was a wonderland to Spot, every day it provided an orchestra of odours to be sampled, enjoyed, and, at times, eaten. With this new animal he was ready to dart back if this strange-looking creature proved dangerous. He had seen birds with beaks like that before and knew enough to keep his distance.

'There you are, Tom. Spot likes him already.'

'How do you know it's a him? Might be a her.'

49

'That means I must give the penguin a name which will do either. I think ... I know. Podge. It's a real podge.'

So the new pet joined the family and settled in happily. Most of the time Podge just stood around, peering at everything and eating fish sparingly. Matt thought it was like many kinds of sea animals, eating when food was plentiful and laying down layers of fat for the lean times.

However Podge was not house-trained and soon the floor of the hut became white with bird droppings.

'More like Splodge than Podge,' Tom was disgusted. 'See you clean up that mess every day, or else you'll have to keep your pet among the fowls. They're all birds and should be happy together.'

After cleaning the floor for a few days Matt had to agree and Podge was placed in a small pen on his own with a roof to keep out the rain and dry grass on the floor for a bed. Gradually the penguin's soft black down began to fall off to reveal beautiful feathers. Steely blue-black on the back of the bird, a snowy white front, and last came the crowning glory, a brilliant orange-yellow crest which hung over its eyes like a fringe.

Matt was triumphant. 'Just look at that. What a beauty. It must be the most beautiful penguin in the world.'

Even Tom agreed it was a handsome bird.

The boys realised that the penguin had been moulting and that was why it hadn't been hungry. Now Podge was ravenous and came eagerly to accept the offerings of fish. Soon it learned to waddle along with the boys and Spot. The dog was happy to accept their new companion, and after a few pecks had established that this was a creature that would not tolerate any fooling about.

Now and again Podge would make a loud braying call. Then one day it approached Matt, whom it had obviously decided to accept as a partner. It held out its paddle-shaped wings, threw its head back and gave a continuous sonorous bray. Matt decided to mimic what the bird was doing, kneeling on the ground, throwing out his arms and doing his best to imitate the call. Tom thought this hilarious. Most days the pair would perform their display to the entertainment of all. Spot often joined in by barking in a frenzy, dancing about the pair, but Podge treated this with disdain. As Matt explained to Tom, penguins were friendly and Podge would fret unless he had company.

Podge really loved the beach. Although slow on land, in the water the penguin could leave both the boys for dead in swimming and diving. Sometimes it would catch a fish, but most of the time it accepted the daily hand-out from Matt.

Podge was the first of many pets Matt gathered about the hut. Scraps of meat brought magpies to the hut door and after a meal they would carol cheerfully in the trees, a chorus which both boys loved. Tom built a bird feeding tray on a pole he drove into the ground. On this they put all kinds of scraps, and sometimes a few grains of sugar or honey, although their supply of these had to be treated carefully.

chapter six

UPS AND DOWNS

ften on a Sunday the boys would take the boat to Goose Island to fish. This Sunday they were tired. It had been a long row with no wind to fill the sail and make the crossing easier. Lunch was damper and wallaby meat, the scraps thrown to Spot. All three stretched out on the headland. It was a day of rest and soon all were asleep.

Half an hour later Spot was on his feet, hair abristle. His deep growl roused Tom. 'Wake up, Matt. Wake up!'

Matt stretched and slowly rose to his feet. It had been a lovely dream with Dad coming to Home Island at last. What a lot he had to tell his father. Then came the reality, he was on Goose Island, with Home Island on the horizon.

Tom pointed. 'Look Matt! Out there!'

Then Matt saw the dolphins. From the north, from the south, from the east and from the west they came in pairs, dipping through the blue water in graceful arcs to form a great circle. The larger animals were on the outer edge, almost as though they were on guard.

Then the double circle spun like a vast wheel. The sea was calm, the silver gulls silent. A dolphin swam into the centre of the ring, leaped high into the air and fell back with a splash which echoed around the bay. Another joined it, then another until there was a foam of movement. The first pair moved off to the open sea while the rest re-formed the circle.

So it went on, each frenzy ending with that pair moving away while the others re-formed the ring. As each couple left, moving towards the horizon, the circle became smaller and smaller. Then it was over. The dolphin school now only a blue-grey shadow in the distance.

'Wow!' exclaimed Tom. 'What on earth was that all about? Wake up, Matt. Don't moon. What do you think they were doing?'

'I don't know,' Matt said slowly, with a puzzled frown on his face. 'Perhaps ... they were dancing.'

'Dancing!' Tom's scorn was plain. 'You're mad. Fish don't dance. Well, we'd better get back home. We've got lots to do before Dad gets back.'

Matthew turned away, his look of wonderment slowly fading. 'But when is Dad coming back? Is he ever coming?'

'Of course he is.' Tom was confident. They both stared out at the western channel between Goose and Home Islands. Their father's small ship must soon sail in, laden with goods from the port of Albany, and the stores they would need.

Back on Home Island not every day was exciting. The boys bagged more and more salt. They became heartily sick of this and only their fear of their father's anger kept them hard at work.

Trapping tammars was a chore, but they had become used to trapping possums back in Albany so it was like the old days. Looking after the hens and the vegetable garden was also like it was back home.

They had become tired of carrying water from the well Somers had dug near the creek. They dug another well near the hut which also gave plenty of water and got rid of one boring job.

Matt collected everything. His museum overflowed with shells, feathers, beetles, birds' eggs, rocks that looked good, sea urchins, shark eggs and cuttlefish bones.

Tom went out with the gun and as his skill improved so did his catch of rock wallabies. The skins were valuable and he looked forward to hearing his father's praise.

A backdrop to both work and play was the roar of the sea. It invaded their dreams and any change woke them up immediately. The swell beat on their beach without ceasing. Then came a day and night they would never forget. First they saw the wispy cirrus clouds which usually came before a storm. Gradually these thickened and, at the same time, the swell became larger and beat on the shore with an awesome, unceasing roar. The land shook with the pounding. The wind rose and the boys took to the shelter of their hut. The storm was rising to full strength. The hut's walls bulged. The wind howled and all around they heard the crashing noise of falling branches. The noise was deafening. The hut shook when a giant tree fell.

Matt was frightened. Tom was just as worried but he knew he was in charge. 'Don't worry. Dad built this hut strong enough to stand any blow. Let's have something to eat. That stew smells good. Warm it up and cut a bit of damper too.'

The old routine was calming. Soon Matt was at work, and they felt better after the meal.

They thought they would never sleep but, tired out, they lay on their beds, and finally the roar outside became part of their dreams.

When the boys awoke the darkness had faded. They went outside. All was calm, and a clear patch of sky perched overhead. Around them was a mad tangle of fallen trees and branches.

'The fowl yard,' cried Matt. The boys ran into the forest but although a branch had fallen on the roof the fowls inside looked happy, pecking at bits of debris which had fallen inside their yard. Podge was safe with them. Even the vegetable garden was undamaged, protected by the surrounding forest.

Suddenly Tom looked up and cried out. 'Matt. Look at the birds. The sky is full of them.'

The blue patch was almost black again with birds: shearwaters gliding, gulls beating their wings and, higher, swifts cutting the air with sickle wings. Higher still a flotilla of pelicans soared majestically. And there were other birds the boys had never seen before, probably land birds from the mainland blown offshore.

Birds must be the brothers of the wind, Matt thought. *Storms don't trouble them. They're part of the air and move with it.*

Then the wind came again. First with a soft touch, then rising to storm level, finally shrieking at cyclone strength. By this time the boys were safe inside the hut, door tightly latched. They settled to breakfast. Stew and damper once more, but at least they knew the hut would stand. It had survived the dreadful night storm.

Late that afternoon the wind finally dropped. They ran to Home Beach to see what had been washed ashore. Here was a treasure trove. All the plants and animals of the seabed had been torn away by the waves which angrily had battered the coast. Lines of foam covered sand and rocks, hiding other trophies. The boys decided they would search again the next day.

Tomorrow they would collect the riches the sea had brought them, just as Somers had told them they should do. Slowly they walked to the hut thinking of their father.

'I hope Dad is somewhere safe,' said Tom. 'That was a bad storm.'

Matt looked at Tom, saucer-eyed. 'He *must* be all right, mustn't he?'

'I'm sure he found shelter in a bay somewhere. He knows the weather signs. He taught them to us.' Tom spoke confidently and kept his fears to himself.

The boys went to bed that night very troubled, unable to stop thinking of the *Silver Gull* battling the storm.

Days passed and the storm winds became nothing more than an exciting memory. They went fishing off the point and struck a school of tommy roughs, so many that as soon as the line hit the water a fish took the bait. They gutted dozens of the victims and strung them on a line to take back to the hut. Matt threw a few small ones back into the sea.

Suddenly there was a rush of a blue-grey body, a fin broke the water, then another. Two dolphins rolled their way to the fragments, accepting them with what looked like a happy grin.

'Look,' shouted Matt. 'Our dolphins are back. I wonder if they're some of those we saw from Goose Island.'

Tom looked sourly at the animals. 'Lucky they didn't come earlier. They scare fish. Greedy blighters. I bet they eat more in a day than we catch in a week.'

'Oh, come on,' protested Matt. 'We catch plenty of fish. They're beautiful.' And before Tom could stop him he unthreaded a fish and threw it near the dolphin. A luminous eye studied Matt, then looked at the fish and swallowed it.

Matt unthreaded another fish, stripped off his shirt and trousers and walked into the water.

'Come back,' shouted Tom. 'Dolphins have teeth you know.'

'I know,' Matt shouted back, 'but they attack sharks so I like them.'

He swam to the dolphins while Tom watched with dismay. Matt was a great know-all but he had better swim out too, just in case. The dolphins circled, then one came towards Matt who was holding out the fish, a flash of peg-like teeth and the fish had gone, disappearing down the pink gullet.

'I'll get another fish,' cried Matt and swam to the shore.

Tom watched the dolphins. They came closer and one brushed against his skin. The body felt like cool velvet. He saw it smile, and smiled back. Then Matt returned with a fish.

'My turn. Give me the fish,' ordered Tom. He held it out to the nearest dolphin and again the gift was accepted.

'Get half-a-dozen fish this time,' ordered Tom.

Soon a new game began. The boys would splash, the

dolphins would come in and take a fish. A few minutes later they would do it all over again. They repeated this until all the fish had gone.

Swimming to the nearest animal Tom gently gripped the slippery back fin and Matt followed with the other dolphin. The animals took off. It was a wild ride but as soon as the dolphins had taken them well away from the shore the boys let go to begin the long swim back. Their new friends followed as though eager to continue the game. Then as suddenly as it had started it was all over. The dolphins leaped high into the air, fell with a splash, then moved out to sea, their bodies rising and falling in a smooth rhythm.

Tom and Matt walked back to the hut in a fever of excitement. What a day! What a life! Who would ever believe the story of the dolphins?

chapter seven

SEALERS

ummer slowly slid into autumn. The boys added blankets to their beds and logs to the fireplace. Both were growing stronger and taller with swimming, walking, climbing, shovelling salt, digging the garden and the hundred-and-one other activities on their Home Island.

'Feel that, Matt. Like iron.' Proudly Tom showed his biceps.

'Feel mine too, Tom. Like iron,' responded Matt.

'Not bad,' agreed Tom but he still looked proudly at his own.

At winter's beginning the rollers started to pound more heavily on the beach. All the old cloud signs appeared and the boys knew they were in for another big blow. They went to bed happy their hut would be safe.

They were awakened with a rude shock as rain poured in on Matt's bed. 'I'm getting wet,' he complained.

'Shift to Dad's bed,' growled Tom. 'There's nothing

to do 'til dawn. Then we can see about fixing the roof. It's only a bit of paperbark and wattle blown away. Easily fixed.'

Matt crawled shivering into the cold bed. He was glad to see the dawn light although heavy clouds shut off the sunrise. Soon the boys were hard at work adding sheets of paperbark to the roof as well as a layer of wattle sticks. The daub would have to wait until the rain stopped. They stoked up the fire with dry logs and sat drinking tea and eating hot stew and potatoes. Their little world was snug but by midday Tom had waited long enough.

'Come on, Matt, let's see what's been happening on the beach.'

They took down their makeshift raincoats, large hessian sacks folded to make a cape, and dropped them over their heads. First, they visited the snares to bring in the night's catch. Few animals were trapped. The wild night had kept the tammars under shelter.

It rained almost every day during the rest of the winter. The boys were miserable but the heavy rain meant there was no salt rim on Pink Lake and both were glad to stop that work.

Where was Somers? He should have been back by the end of autumn. A gnawing worry haunted the boys. Still, picking up cargoes was a chancy business and he had warned them it might be six months before he came back.

It seemed to the boys that time was passing more slowly. Even fishing was not as exciting as it used to be, and they had not been able to get the dolphins to come and play. Matt no longer leaped out of bed eagerly each morning to get breakfast, then run on the beach to see what he could find. Tom was becoming more sullen.

The island was becoming a prison, where they were doing hard labour.

What's gone wrong? thought Matt. He was sitting in front of the fire after the evening meal. Tom had gone straight to his bunk without saying a word. Matt sat poking the fire and hoping Somers would come soon.

Suddenly Spot rose and growled.

'What's up, Spot? Tom, look at Spot. He's heard something.'

Tom rose on his elbow, stared at Spot then reached for the gun under his bed.

What could be out there? Fear as tangible as the darkness filled the hut. The dim light from the fire threw frightening shadows.

'Open up! Be quick about it,' called a harsh voice.

No! thought Matt, but then he realised they had no choice, the intruder could break down the door.

Tom jumped out of bed and shifted the wooden bar.

A dozen men poured in. The bearded faces looked grim. The boys had no trouble recognising them as sealers. They had a fearsome reputation in Albany. Then two more came in, carrying another man on a rough stretcher. They lowered him on to their father's bed.

'Poor bastard,' said one of the sealers. 'Bitten by a seal. Got him in both knees. Stupid old Sam not watching out for the klapmatch when he was killing her pup. She bit him good and proper.'

'Could have been worse,' laughed another weasel-faced individual. 'Could have bitten him on the bum or worse still, taken off a more important bit.' They all laughed.

A tall, burly man growled, 'Stow it. Look lads, we're busy with the seals on the western island. Look after old Sam for us. We should be back in a couple of weeks to pick him up. Sam should be better by then.'

'Or dead,' said Weaselface, the gang humorist.

'Keep his wounds clean and feed him. When we come back we'll give you something for your trouble.'

He turned to the joker. 'Keep your trap shut or I'll shut it for you.' Then he turned to Tom and asked, 'Anything we can bring you?'

'Yes,' said Tom quickly, having lost his fear. 'We could do with a lance for spearing fish.'

'Good,' said the leader looking at him with new interest. 'We'll see you soon. Somers' sons aren't you — heard you were on the island.'

The sealers strode off into the darkness as swiftly as they had come. The boys heard their voices die away. They heard a boat being dragged over the sand, the rattle of oars, and then there was silence. Even the man on the bed made no sound and Spot had relaxed.

Tom wrinkled his nose at the strong smell from the sealer. 'They must have knocked him out with rum. Well, we might as well go back to sleep and see what happens in the morning.'

For a time Matt lay awake. How can we look after the man? What will happen if he dies? Will the sealers come back and what will they say if he is dead? Will they blame us? When will Dad come back? The questions rattled around in his head. Finally, he fell asleep.

With the coming of the sun Matt stirred the fire alight and decided to cook some porridge. They hadn't bothered much with this but it should be good for a sick man. Or at least he hoped so.

The bustle woke Sam. He stared around the hut in surprise then asked, 'And what will be the names of you lads?'

'I'm Matthew and that's Tom on the bed. That's Spot. Your mates left you here last night and asked us to look after you.'

'Ah! You'll be Somers' boys. We heard you were to make your home on the island. And good English names you've both got. So you're going to look after me. I'll soon be off your hands. Old Sam won't be kept in bed for long, just from a couple of bites from a bad-tempered klapmatch. Bad cess to her.'

'Klapmatch? What's that?' asked Matt.

'A female, boy. A female seal. It was a klapmatch that bit me. And I wasn't troubling her.'

'But weren't you killing her baby?' asked Matt with some surprise.

'And what's wrong with that? Didn't God put man on this earth to have dominion over the fish of the sea and over the fowl of the air, and over cattle and over all the earth, and everything that creepeth upon the earth? The offering of God, Matthew, and not be lightly let go. You look at me surprised, but I was once a boy like you. Learned my prayers and read my Bible. The Good Book is never far from my side. I always carry it with me.' He dragged out of his huge coat pocket a tattered and grimy Bible.

'Ah boys, if only Adam had listened to God and not Eve we'd still be living in the Garden of Eden. And I wouldn't be an Ishmael, a wanderer on the face of the earth, forced to live with evil men who laugh at God's words. Yet there will be a reckoning.' Old Sam lifted his eyes to the roof of the hut and fell silent.

'Would you like some porridge, Sam?' asked the practical Tom.

'I would lad. I would. Stick to the sides of my stomach it looks, if I'm any judge.'

He tasted the plateful Matt put in his hands and ate eagerly.

'Not bad, young Tom. Indeed I might say very good. And now for a drink of water to wet my whistle.'

'I'll get some fresh from the well,' said Matt, hurrying out. He came back quickly with a brimming pannikin. Sam took a huge swallow, then spat it all over the bed.

'What tricks are you playing with me lad? Don't dare cross Sam. Get some decent drinking water and do it quick,' and he glared savagely at the surprised and fearful Matt.

'But it's fresh from the well,' protested Matt. 'We drink it all the time. We dug the well ourselves near the hut. The one Dad made was too far away.'

'Idiot boys. It's a wonder you're still alive. This water is salt. Brackish anyhow. Not fit for man nor beast. Now run and get me some from the well your Dad dug.'

Matt ran fast and came back minutes later, breathless but with the pannikin full once more. Sam sipped carefully, then took a long drink.

'Ah, that's the stuff. Better than all the grog in the world. But tell me, have you been drinking that other stuff for long?'

'Yes,' the boys replied in unison.

'And how do you feel?'

'Not good,' admitted Tom. 'We've been poorly for the last month or so.'

'Bad-tempered too.' Matt spoke with feeling, remembering the cuffs he had got from Tom.

'Of course you've been poorly and bad-tempered,' exclaimed Sam. 'You're poisoned with salt water. I'll be bound that well of yours is too shallow and too near the sea. So fill it in. It's been changing so gradually like, you never noticed it. It's lucky for you boys that seal bit me. A few more weeks of that muck and you'd have been really ill. You see boys, God moves in mysterious ways. My mates left me, a sick man on your hands, but it was you who were sick and I'll make you better.'

He beamed at them, pleased they were now in his debt, rather than the other way round.

'What about a mug of tea? Then we can take a look at those legs of mine. You can put some of that salt water from your well into a can to warm on the fire, Matt. Salty water never hurts on your outside, no matter how bad it is for your innards. And some clean rags too, if you have them.'

The boys ran to do his bidding. He was no longer a frightening, scowling sealer with a black beard and flashing eyes but a jovial friend, a kind of replacement father. Matt gave him a mug of strong hot tea with plenty of sugar while Tom cleaned the seal bites as well as he could, sponging them with warm water. The wounds didn't look deep and there was no redness near the bite so he guessed Sam would be up and about within a week or two. They put new bandages in place and left Sam while they went to inspect their snares.

'Look,' said Matt, gazing back at the hut where he could see Sam sitting near the open door, immersed in his Bible.

Tom nodded. 'He's all right.'

As the days passed Sam kept them enthralled with tales of whales and whalers, seals and sealers. Often he spoke of the chase of right whales and how Home Island had once been a base for the hunters.

'Right whales?' asked Matt.

'Ay lad. The right whale for us to catch. Many whales,

once they die, sink to the bottom and are lost. Not the right whale. She floats when killed and is full of oil. So that makes it the right whale for us. Some whales are too fast or too big for us to catch. Some are too dangerous unless you have a good crew. That's the sperm whale, Leviathan, the Bible talks about.'

'Moby Dick,' cried Matt.

'Moby duck?' asked Sam. 'Never heard of that bird.'

'Moby Dick,' explained Matt. 'It was the great white whale which killed Ahab and sank his ship.'

'Never heard of Ahab, not on the Australian run,' replied Sam with a puzzled frown.

'How could a whale sink a ship?' scoffed Tom. 'Rowboat maybe, like those you use when hunting, but not a big ship.'

Sam stared at him under bristling brows. 'That's how little you know, me lad. Wait 'til you see a sperm whale bearing down on your boat with its great mouth open, full of teeth ready to grab you. Most whalers do come back from their three or four year run but the unlucky ones leave their bones behind.' Again he glared at both boys. 'Never laugh at the sea. Never scoff at the giants of the ocean. All men on whaleboats respect the big whales. Yes, Matt,' he said, turning to the boy, 'your Moby Dick must have been one of the big sperm bulls. Too strong to kill.'

'Oh,' said Matt. 'I'm sorry. Moby Dick was in a story.'

'Written by someone who'd never been to sea I'll be bound,' laughed Sam.

'No, he spent two years on a whaler. It's a marvellous book.'

'Ah, I could write a book meself if I had the trick of putting the words down on paper,' said Sam. 'I well remember one day in the Pacific we got among a pod of sperm whales. We thought our fortunes were made and we might fill our casks with oil and be home two years earlier.

'The skipper was in one of the boats and I was in another, with four more spread among the whales. Then one of the men shouted and we all turned to look. A giant bull charged the ship again and again. Slowly she heeled over and was gone.' He paused. 'There was nothing we could do but watch.'

'Why did the whale attack the ship?' Tom asked.

'That's the puzzle. The first whale we struck was a mother with her calf. She may have been the old bull's favourite. Perhaps he was just in a bad temper. Who knows the mind of Leviathan? I tell you when you come near a sperm whale just before the strike, with your harpoon, and he fixes you with that calm eye of his, you know fear. I'm not too proud to admit it.'

'What happened then?' asked Tom, curious as to the fate of the sealers.

'It was bad,' confessed Sam. 'Our boats went to the spot where the ship sank and picked up some survivors who were swimming. Not many because most seamen don't know how to swim.'

'Why not?' asked Tom. He and Matt could swim almost before they could walk.

'Ah boys. Just think of a seaman falling from the mast into the sea or washed overboard in a storm, or his ship sinking. There's no hope of rescue, and if you can swim, that only means you take longer to drown. Increase the pain. Anyhow we kept together for a few days, then a storm came and we were separated. Luckily a couple of days later most of us were found by another whaler. They'd lost men so were glad to sign us on. The only other boat that was picked up was the captain's.

Sam shuddered. 'He lived.' He stared into the fire.

'And did any of the others survive with him?'

'One boy.'

'But what happened to the rest of the seamen in the boat?' persisted Tom.

'Ah lad, whaling is a tough life. You've only been on this island for a few months. Imagine four years cooped up in a small whaling ship. Perhaps thirty or forty men, and some not as good as they should be. Rough men. Evil men. But they rub along well enough in a general sort of way. I've never heard of mutiny on a whaler because we were all free to speak our mind and we worked as a team. And the excitement. There we'd be rowing like madmen to where we thought the whale would come up to spout. Quiet we were then. It was like a tiger stalking a deer. So quiet.'

Tom was a bulldog when he wanted to know something. 'But what happened to the men in the captain's boat?'

Sam knocked the dregs from his pipe into the fire, cut more tobacco, rammed it home with his horny thumb then reached for an ember from the fire to light up.

'Ah well, best I tell you so you'll know this can be a hard world. When the captain and the boy were found, in their pockets, man and boy alike, there were bits of flesh. Human flesh. When men are starving they forget God's laws and turn cannibal.'

Sam was silent and Tom shivered. He wished he hadn't asked, yet there was a queer sort of thrill in thinking of the boat alone on the ocean.

'But those were the few bad days in my whaling life. There were more good ones. Always a chance to make money. And there was the chase. You haven't lived until you've been on a whale chase. Or on a whaling ship. Good they were. Some been afloat for fifty years and still sound as a bell. They might look clumsy with their three masts, blunt bows and cut-off sterns but they were built to handle the roaring forties like a duck in a pond. Any wind, any waves, and we would ride them. Flying like an albatross we left to the clipper ships. Slow and steady was our way.

'Each whaler carried half a dozen small boats we could row. Well built, lovely craft and I've pulled many a weary mile in them. You may not think so looking at me now but I was a head harpooner in those days. Specksynders they called us. We were the cream of the ship. We slept away from the others, aft with the officers. If we couldn't strike true once we sighted the whale then everyone would lose.'

'Thar she blows,' shouted Matt, carried away by the old man's story.

'You need sharp eyes in the crow's nest to see not only the spout but what kind of whale it is.'

'Can you tell just from the spout?' Matt wondered.

'Of course, my boy. Poor show if you couldn't. No good wasting time on the blue whale, old sulphur-bottom we called it with its bright, yellow belly. A big blue would break free in the end and all you'd have for your trouble was aching arms, lost rope and a lost harpoon. But when we saw a right whale then it was all boats in the water. We pulled with the steersmen screaming like madmen, urging us on. And how we pulled. We flew through the water. It was money for all if we won, and empty pockets if we lost. It was a sad crew if it went home after three years at sea with half-empty oil barrels. Yes, we were happy ships. Crew was all mixed, came from a dozen different countries.'

'How did you understand each other?' puzzled Matt.

'We rubbed along. All of us had some English and a bit of any language you might meet on the high seas. Even the Aborigines picked up new words quickly.'

'Aborigines?' said Tom in surprise. 'What good were they?'

'Aborigines and South Sea Islanders were among the best. I always felt safe in a boat with them.'

'And were the catching boats dangerous?' Matt asked.

'I'll say they were. Nearly seven hundred yards of rope — good rope too. The best hemp could take a strain of five tons, enough to hold most whales but the king of them all, the blue. All that rope was coiled in a tub or perhaps two in the stern near the steersman with the end running forward to the harpoon. Away we would row after the whale. When it sounded it was not easy to guess where it might come up again. Many a weary chase ended with nothing.'

Sam spat in the fire then took another pull on his pipe.

'But there would be the times when the steersman would call to me and I would stand up with the harpoon, proud and tall, ready for the throw. I tell you that was a grand moment. Every man holding his breath and a silence like death. Then Leviathan rose, the deep sigh of its breath pouring warm and moist over me. Ah the feeling when I struck true and the giant felt the bite of my good iron. Then all hell would break loose. We rushed away like a bolting horse. It was then you had to look smart. Get a loop of rope around your foot and you'd be tossed into the sea and be dragged to your death when the whale sounded. A loop around your neck and death was quicker. I can tell you on a whaleboat it was watch out, step lively and pull hard!'

Sam fell silent, lost in a dream of golden, olden days when he was the king of the boat.

'What happened when you struck and the whale took off?' persisted Tom.

'My job was done for a bit. I took the steersman's place as we went off on a Nantucket sleigh ride.' He laughed. 'American talk. Nantucket was the home of the best whalers, and if the whale was away dragging us over the sea we had a wild ride. Nothing like it I know on land or sea. Though I've never been on a sleigh so that might be just as exciting.

'Sometimes the whale sounded, going deep and staying, sullen. Then it would come up like a rocket under you. That's the moment you'd never forget. Nothing you can do. Just like a giant hand coming from the depths and up goes boat, men, oars, rope, tubs in one great heave, and there we were, all in the water with Leviathan thrashing a giant tail, perhaps killing a man in its flurry. Many a mate I lost that way.'

He paused for reflection. 'You see lads, the sea is the home of the whale and we are only visitors.'

'And what comes at the end?' Tom prompted.

'When we get close enough we use iron lances to weaken the whale. As the minutes pass we watch until finally it raises the red flag.'

'Red flag?' asked Tom.

'A great spray of red pours out of the blowhole. Then we know blood has got into its lungs. The fight will soon be over. Then comes the long haul, either to the beach if you're a bay whaler working from the land, or back to the ship if you're on the high seas. Then we cut the blubber loose with great knives. Tiring work that.

Then comes trying.'

Sam held up his hand. 'Yes boy, I know what you're going to ask. Trying is heating the blubber to get out the oil. We used giant pans called trypots. There are a few cracked ones left on Home Beach. This place used to be the home of the western bay whalers. A great place it was in those days too. You've seen the ruins of the huts. When the barrels were full it was sails set and head for home.'

'Where's home for you?' asked Tom.

'That's a question. I was born in England of an English father and an Irish mother. Fell on evil ways as a boy and came out with an assisted passage.'

The boys smiled.

'You can smile but it was a cruel government that sent me out for stealing food for my young brothers. But the judge did me a good turn. Mum and Dad and all my kin died, some starving, some from illness. Home is here. Anywhere I sleep for the night. I'm a wanderer. This country has been good to me. I've had grand times, but it's a comedown to be a bloody sealer instead of a whaling man.'

'What about sharks?' asked Tom who wanted to know more about the exciting times.

'A good dig with my lance finished most sharks. But not the great white death. It's a bit like your Moby Dick. Sends shivers down my spine I can tell you. You lance it time and time again and it still comes back, chopping great chunks out of the dead whale. Waste of oil, too, and we didn't like that.' He spat in the fire. 'But land sharks are worse.'

'Land sharks?' both boys cried out.

'Yes, land thieves. They wait 'til a poor seaman is drunk, then slit his throat for a few sovereigns. Money he's earned hard through years at sea!'

'Do you know if a whaler really hid some gold on this island?' asked Matt.

Sam laughed. 'I did hear that story and lots more like it. But ... Peter did die here, and I heard he asked his mates to bury him near his hut. His grave must be somewhere near those ruins, covered with bush I suppose. If there was any gold his mates would have had a good look for it. That's enough talking. It's time for sleep. My mates might be back tomorrow. I hope they've made a good killing.'

He looked at his knees. 'As clean a bit of healing as I've ever had. You boys make good nurses and good cooks and good listeners. But I'll be glad to be back in my hut on Seal Island. Made it myself out of wattle and daub just like you. A great fireplace. It never smokes and it's a snug little place. I suppose that's my home,' he said in some surprise. 'Goodnight boys.'

Sam was right. Next morning a sail appeared on the western horizon and soon the sealer's ship was racing into the bay.

But when was Somers coming?

chapter eight

THE SEAL HUNT

he excitement of Sam's stay gradually died away. The boys went back to hard work. Somers would be returning soon and everything must be ready for the house they were to build, big enough for each of them to have their own room.

Tom found a thicket of trees which seemed almost as though grown for the job. All were about ten feet high with a stem no thicker than his thumb. *It was probably a plantation which came up after a fire*, he thought. The trunks were clean with only a tuft of leaves on the top.

The boys knew that after every fire thousands of seedlings came up after the next rain. Thriving in the ash bed, they all grew towards the light, keeping pace with their fellows. From above, the forest almost looked like a lawn, with the treetops a flat carpet of green. They cut hundreds of the trees and stored them near the hut.

'Enough to build a mansion', claimed Matt.

Old Sam had told them about club trees and had shown them where they grew. These were shrubs, much sought after by sealers, as the trunks were short, about six feet long and twice as thick as wattles. The root-stock formed an almost perfect ball underground. When dug out, with the stem trimmed to make a handle, these became perfect clubs. Sam said they used them for killing seals, and if the boys dug enough and let them season in the shade ready for the sealer's next visit, they would be well paid for their work.

The boys still explored the island, always on the look out for treasures. They turned over all the stones near the ruins of the whalers' huts but with no success. Matt thought of the right whale and humpback mothers who once came into Home Bay to give birth to their young. In the safety of these waters, at least until the whalers came, the mothers suckled their babies for months until they were strong enough to travel south to the great feeding grounds of the Antarctic seas.

Tom was keen to find the whaler's rumoured hoard of gold.

They found an old grave, with a rough wooden cross. Matt cleared away the weeds, then helped with the search but they found nothing.

They also looked for another kind of treasure. Sam had reminded them of ambergris, the strange stuff found in the stomachs of sperm whales that was worth a fortune in the city where it was used in the making of perfumes. Everyone knew about ambergris in Albany, and a few lucky finders had made a fortune even from small lumps.

Sam had told them of a sperm whale which came to the Rubbing Rocks in the bay. The whalers had given the rocks this name because the giants of the sea came to the smooth rocks, awash at low tide, to scrape against the hard surfaces. Perhaps they got rid of barnacles which grew on their bodies, just as they did on ship bottoms. Weed growths could also be scraped away. Perhaps they liked to scratch, just like humans who leaned against verandah posts to rub themselves.

One day the whalers saw a large sperm whale rubbing against the rocks. Six boats pulled out but it made no attempt to escape. When harpooned, instead of sounding and leading them on a wild ride, it swam for a short distance, then hoisted the red flag, turning on its back as it died. Triumphantly they towed it ashore to tap the oil in the head. When the body was cut open they could see the whale had been sick, and they found a huge lump of ambergris, almost a fifth of a ton. When their ship reached London they sold this for twenty thousand pounds.

Sam's stories had given the boys new interest in searching along the beaches, but ambergris was not the only lure. The roaring forties brought a great deal of flotsam and jetsam from the sea. There were twenty-foot long stalks of seaweed thrown on the sand, logs which may have come from South Africa or South America, and dead seabirds from tiny storm petrels to a giant wandering albatross. There were thousands of shells, and Matt's collection of the rare and the beautiful became bigger and bigger.

Always they wondered, *Where is Dad?* Already he was more than three months late. Day after day passed and the boys became more and more despondent.

At last a sail appeared. The strong wind brought the ship around the point into Home Bay under full press of sail. Joy turned to disappointment. It was not the

Silver Gull, only the sealers back once more — as they had promised.

The ship anchored and the men rowed ashore full of good humour after a successful hunt. The hold was packed with sealskins, not of hair seals but the much more valuable fur seals. The boys ran along the sand to meet them.

'Hullo Sam! Good to see you. How are the legs? No more klapmatch bites?' shouted Matt.

Sam's eyes slid away as he mumbled. 'All right Matt. Good as gold. Glad to see you. Looking fit and well too. Not drinking any salt water now?'

'No fear. We use the old well. We filled in the other one. We've so much to show you.' He grabbed Sam by the hand to drag him towards the hut.

'Hold it,' Bill, the leader, called. 'We've something we must tell you. Bloody sorry we're the ones to bring the bad news.'

Tom and Matt stared at him.

'Met a boat from Salisbury Island. They had just sailed from Albany. They told us the news.'

'What news?' The boys inhaled sharply, then held their breath. They guessed what was coming.

'Your Dad. On his way to Home Island. Got caught in that big blow a month ago. A lee shore and he went aground. The ship broke up on a reef.'

'But how did they know?' asked Tom, still hoping.

'Found bits of the wreck on the beach first. Then the stern board with the name *Silver Gull*. Last of all they found your Dad's body. Buried him on the headland so he could look out towards Home Island. It was the best they could do.'

'They did it right,' volunteered Sam. 'Put up a cross too. You can go and see the place one day. Perhaps this trip, and then you can say goodbye to your Dad. A good man by all accounts, and much respected along the coast.'

The boys were silent, eyes filling with tears. The sealers watched them.

'Come on, lads,' the leader said. He tried to take Matt in a rough embrace, to steady him as the boy's body trembled with shock. Matt shook himself free and ran off along the beach, tears blinding him. Tom followed. He, too, was numb with shock and he stumbled as he walked.

Sam called after them, 'We'll get a meal for you lads. Come back when you're ready. No hurry. We can look after ourselves.'

The boys sat on the beach together. They could not believe they would never see Somers again. He would never see what they had done. All their hard work, the skins, the salt, the log, the garden ...

'What will we do? We're marooned here. Nobody will come for us,' muttered Tom.

Matt stared at his brother in dismay. 'Of course they will. Ships call in. Whalers, sealers, fishermen, perhaps even a yacht. Somebody will. We've got things worth selling. Skins, salt. That will pay for our passages to Albany, and we can work. I'm sure Dad's friends will look after us.'

'More likely the orphanage,' said Tom.

The orphanage. The gloomy house on the hill where boys and girls rarely mixed with the other children. It was a place to scare anyone.

'We're too old for that, aren't we?' queried Matt.

Tom did not answer. He did not know. After a long time he said, 'I'm going home, Matt. I'm hungry.'

'You can't. Not with the sealers there. You know

they'll take us back to their island. I don't like them, except old Sam.'

'Don't be an idiot. They're only men. A bit rough but they mean well. Come on, Matt. We can't stay out here for ever and starve to death.'

It was chilly as the sun sank behind the trees and reluctantly Matt stood up. Slowly the two boys walked back along the beach to the hut. A steady stream of smoke from the chimney promised both warmth and a hot meal. The sealers greeted them with subdued cheerfulness. Hot mugs of tea were pushed into their hands and a large bowl of stew followed.

Bill left them to their meal and turned to Sam.

'Well. Do you think there are enough seals in that rookery below the hill to make it worth a trip to the western end?' he asked.

'Too right,' agreed Sam. 'But it'll be a tricky landing. That's where the big swell comes in. Rough going. We may have to swim the skins to the boat.'

One of the men who had been sitting in silence jeered.

'You always were a jeremiah, Sam. Always expecting the worst. When have any of us been scared of getting wet? If they're good skins, I say let's get them.'

Sam looked up in contempt. 'What's the good of getting skins and drowning on the way back to the boats? When you're as old as I am you may get some sense but I doubt it.'

Tempers flared. The sealing gang was a lawless group who accepted a leader only if he could fight better and think better than any of the others. Bill stood up and glared around until all were silent.

'Sam, is there anywhere some of us can land to cut off the seals before they get to the water? We want more than pups.'

'I only saw the rookery from the top of the hill and it was a long way off.' Sam thought for a moment. 'At a guess I'd say there would be about fifty harems of klap-matches ruled over by old wigs.'

Bill whistled. 'That means two-and-a-half thousand seals, not to mention the pups. There should be plenty of them at this time of year. Spring is always good.'

He turned to Tom and Matt. 'Well boys, it should be a good day tomorrow. If you throw in your lot with us, you'll get your share of skins. We've been using your food and your hut and you can help tomorrow with the hunt. It's your first, so it should be exciting. We'll take all the boats. Sam and you boys can climb to the north side, as near to the hill as you can get. Another party can walk along the beach to cut off the rookery from the sea. Try and wound the pups first so the mothers will stay with them. Leave the wigs to the last. I'll take a couple of men to work the ship so we can get in close and you can swim out with the skins. Sam and the boys can walk back if they like or swim to the boat.'

His look challenged the room but they were cheerful now. A rich load of skins was waiting.

At dawn the camp was astir. The men soon emptied the pot of stew, breaking off lumps of damper to eat with it. They grunted approval of Matt's cooking and cried out that such likely lads would be a good addition to the gang. Then they loaded the killing clubs into the boats, admiring the new ones the boys had made. Bill counted their clubs in a businesslike way. 'That will be two skins apiece for your work boys.'

'Two skins each for a few clubs?' complained one of the men, but he was silenced by a glare from the leader.

'Pipe down, you idiot.'

As excited as a group of children on a picnic they

tumbled into the boats. To them killing days were great days. The spice of danger and the thrill of the chase were added to the thought of the money to be earned.

Boats were hauled on board and the ship moved out to sea. First the skipper landed most of the men well out of sight of the rookery. No warning should reach the seals until the final killing dash. The skipper then began the long haul around the bay, timing his arrival at the rookery for when most of the slaughter would be over.

Sam and the boys had begun early, making the long climb up the hill until they reached a spot near the rookery. The rest of the men came into sight, beginning their hard climb along the coastline, positioning themselves on the shore to cut off any escape of the seals. Sam and the boys would come down the hill as soon as the killing began, to help in finishing off the pups hiding among the rocks.

The boys hurried Sam towards the top of the granite hill.

'Don't show yourselves on the top,' warned Sam. 'Go slow the last few steps and just peer over.'

Every now and again a young wig challenged an old beach master. At each challenge the mothers and babies would scatter. A mixture of bellows and squeals came from all.

Sam began to show his excitement. 'A couple of thousand seals! About forty old wigs — the beach masters — and twice as many young bulls. Now watch this! Here's a brave young bull trying his luck against the master of a harem. He'll be sorry! That's no old man ready for the scrap heap but a tough bull in the prime of life. Just you watch.'

The bull, as big as the beach master, inched his way

towards his quarry. He was pushing aside pups to try and get to the females. The king reared to stare at the challenger. Like a thunderbolt he charged headlong through his harem. Females and pups scattered. The young bull faced the veteran, ready to grip his rival's neck.

They fought breast to breast, trying for a place to grip. The strength and experience of the old male began to tell. The young bull was bleeding from a dozen wounds. Slowly the beach master forced him out of his territory. He fled through other territories, and was slashed at in turn by the resident bulls.

Other challenging males, stimulated by the first fight, charged in turn. The defending bulls rose to meet them. The bellowing, the roars and the squealing added to the clamour. Then the sealers struck. The klap-matches tried to save their babies but the sealers' clubs fell with sickening thuds. High on the hill the boys could hear the sounds.

The terrified colony broke and fled for the sea, leaving behind squealing pups that were easy prey for the sealers, now as excited with bloodlust as had been the bulls. Swinging their clubs in a frenzy they forgot all weariness in a red blaze of slaughter.

Sam had hurried to the killing field but the boys could not move. Matt turned away in horror. His face went green and he vomited on the grass. Soon Tom joined him.

Sam slowly climbed the hill to the boys. He looked at their faces and said quietly. 'A bad business, but life isn't all pretty lads. You'll see more than a few dead seals before you're much older. Come on. We must help. A lot of skinning to do if we're to get back to the hut before dark. We don't want to be out here all night.

There's a bit of weather blowing up.'

The men were hard at work among the rocks which had been the home of the fur seals for thousands of years. The skins were carried to the promontory. Bill had brought in the boats and the prize was ferried back to the ship which was lying at anchor. Often a man and his load would fall into the sea and be hauled back onto the boat. There were hours of backbreaking work.

Then came disaster. One sealer, pushing a bundle of skins before him, screamed in agony. His body flailed the water. A gradually spreading stain made the sea red. A huge fin broke the surface as a great white shark came to the surface. Fish and man disappeared forever.

The other sealers said little. They took great care getting in and out of the boats and none ventured into the sea.

At last the job was done and the men rested for a smoke. Bill and his crew set sail for Home Bay while the rest began the long walk back, this time taking an easier path. The boys were shocked to see how quickly they seemed to have forgotten their dead mate. They walked in silence — thinking again of their father.

Back at the hut the crew was happy.

'A good day,' said Bill. 'This lot should bring in plenty. And there's Pat's share too now he's gone.'

'Not much loss,' said another sealer, with a harsh laugh.

'And there're the boys too,' continued Bill, ignoring the comment. 'They're only boys yet, so only half shares. Everyone agreed?'

There was a growl of assent.

'Now they're part of our team,' said the weasel-faced man, 'it won't be long before they earn their full share.'

'No,' protested Matt. 'We're not part of your team.'

'You soon will be,' asserted Weaselface, staring intently at Matt. 'You'll have to leave Home Island now your dad's dead.'

Dead! The word fell like a hammer blow.

Bill changed the subject in a hurry. 'Pity we had no women with us so we could pick up a few more skins before we return to Seal Island.' He turned to Tom. 'Aborigines are good but the Maoris are the best. Nice and plump. They swim to the rocks holding a club close to their bodies. Then they wriggle ashore, moving slowly towards the seals flat on their bellies. Sometimes they scratch themselves, just like a seal does with its flipper. Lovely they look, with their black bodies glistening, just like a seal.'

Weaselface licked his thin lips.

'Pity we lost those women we had on Kangaroo Island. They don't last,' said another sealer.

'Don't know why ... they go into their sulks. Like a koala on a rope. I had one of those as a pet. It just sat and wouldn't eat the gum leaves I gave it. Black women are the same. They go into their sulks and after a while they die. Still we can get plenty more on the mainland.'

'Boys aren't bad,' asserted another. 'They can wriggle along just as well and you two are brown enough to look like seals. You could easily look like women from a distance.'

'Even better close-up,' leered Weaselface.

Matt shrank away.

'Stow your gab,' growled Sam. 'You've said enough.'

chapter nine

DISASTER!

ight lads. You can start earning your keep,' Bill stated. 'In the morning we'll have a real blow-out. Make plenty of stew. Have plenty of damper too, so we can have breakfast and get away to Seal Island in good time.'

He turned to his men, 'We'll doss on the beach and leave the lads here so they can get the food ready and pack their gear.'

Turning back to the boys he said, 'Bring what you need, lads. We can look at your skins tomorrow and see what to pay you. We'll take the bags of salt too. What we don't want we can sell to other sealers.'

'We'll play fair with you if you play fair with us,' came in a deep rumble from one of them. 'Sealing is the only kind of life for a real man. I leave it to you, Bill. I'm off to the beach.'

The others followed, and the boys were alone in the hut. Both got busy, preparing a mammoth stew that would cook slowly all night on the edge of the coals, and making the dampers, ready for cooking in the morning. While they worked they argued.

'What can we do?' asked Tom. 'Dad's gone. We can't keep on living on our own forever. It may be years before anyone comes here again. I'm sick of having nobody to talk to.'

'You can always talk to me,' replied Matt. 'I could live here forever.'

'You're only a kid. I'm a man and I want to work with men and talk with men. I'm going.'

Matt was silent. He knew Tom wanted to go with the sealers for the adventure, the rough talk and jokes, and the rum. He had not missed the sly meaning of the gap-toothed sealer who had said women and boys were both useful for catching wary seals, and for other things. Somers had often talked about the sealers and their ways.

Tom went to his bunk to dream of a new life, away from Home Island. Matt went to his bunk and worried. He thought they might end up like slaves, at everyone's beck and call. And it would be worse at night when the sealers were full of rum, drunk and dangerous. What would Somers have wanted them to do? Exhausted at last, he fell into an uneasy sleep.

The morning was bright and clear. Home Island had never looked so beautiful. A warm sun gilded the gum tree tips and washed the sand pale yellow. The lake glowed pink. The sealers trooped up to the hut demanding breakfast. The fire was already blazing and the stew hot, while the damper was baking in the coals.

The sealers shouted their appreciation of the cooking and it was all fun as they talked about the new voyage. Any move was a change and they looked forward to having the boys with them as a break in the pattern of their lives. And, their cooking was good.

Matt took the dishes to the beach after the meal, rubbed them clean with sand and rinsed them in the sea before carrying them back to the hut. The men were busy salting and rolling the seal skins. The wallaby skins had been tied into bundles, Bill counted the take and told Tom how much he and Matt would be paid. He was overjoyed. They would soon be rich at this rate.

Then the captain brought out a large bottle, took a swig and passed it on to the next man. At last the bottle reached Tom. He hesitated, then gulped, choking on the fiery liquor. The men cheered and clapped him on the back.

'Good lad. You'll make a sealer yet, but don't hold onto the neck as though you want to strangle it. Keep it moving boy. Give your brother a drink.'

Matt looked at Tom in horror then took to his heels. The sealers laughed and kept the bottle travelling. After the second round it was empty and the last drinker tossed the bottle into the bushes.

'Right,' said Bill. 'That's it. All to the boat and take everything with you. Come on, Tom. Is this your swag? Pick it up and get along.'

'What about Matt?' protested Tom. 'We can't just leave him.'

'Give him a shout.'

Tom shouted until his voice was hoarse but no small figure came out of the bush.

'I'll tell you what,' suggested Bill. 'Write a note to say we'll be back in two weeks. Then you can tell him what life is like in a sealers' camp. If you don't like it after two weeks, you can stay on the island. But if you want to join us and Matt still doesn't want to come he'll just have to stay here and lump it. Some boat will come along and take him back to Albany and the orphanage. That's if he's lucky. More likely he'll be shanghaied by the first ship that comes. Being a ship's boy is a dog's life I can tell you,' he said grimly. 'That's how I started and I wouldn't want to wish that on anybody. So write that note. We're burning daylight and must be off. You can bring the dog if you like,' offered Bill as an extra inducement.

Tom thought for a moment. Bill was talking sense. He nodded and wrote confidently, weighing the note down with a shell from Matt's collection. Then he picked up his swag and ran to the beach. He'd better leave Spot. He would be company for Matt and a fortnight was not long. There was Podge, too. She'd be more company and sometimes he thought Matt cared more for the penguin than for him.

The sealers hallooed as they saw Tom and soon they were rowing towards the ship, lying at anchor in Home Bay. It was a perfect morning. Soon the south-westerly filled the sails and they headed for Seal Island.

Matt came out of the bushes once the ship was well on its way. Both Spot and Podge hurried towards him as though fearing they had been abandoned. He ran back to the hut and read the note.

Back in two weeks. You can come with us then.
Tom

A feeling of sadness came over him as he read the few words. Tom had gone, just like that, with no other message. He hugged Spot and then gave Podge a scratch on her neck feathers. She loved that. He decided to go for a long walk. There seemed no point in doing much work. He would still have to catch wallabies for food as well as go fishing so Podge could have something to eat. But no more bagging salt and no more skins, at least not for a while. He was sick of killing. He took his bag and walked along the southern beach where the thousands of shells jingled under his feet. Storms threw most of their loads onto this shoreline. Finally he came to the cliff which was the marker for the homeward track. It was then he saw a grey lump on the beach.

A grey lump! Was this the famous ambergris, 'ambergrease' as old Sam called it? Feverishly he tried to remember how to tell whether it was the real stuff or just a lump of tallow or whale blubber. It didn't seem to have much smell if it was going to be used for perfume. Still, better be sure than sorry, so he tried to put it into his bag.

It's heavy, too heavy for me to carry, he thought. *If it is ambergris we'll be rich. I'll break it into four or five pieces and take it back to the hut a bit at a time.*

He looked around for something suitable but decided he would need to bring the axe to cut it up. Using a stone he battered one end until a piece broke away, not too heavy to fit into his bag.

Then he forgot all about the ambergris as he stared out to sea. Beyond the line of breakers a school of sperm whales swam slowly along. These were the giants among whales, like Moby Dick of the story. There were about thirty of them. White plumes shot into the air as the animals breathed out. All were about thirty feet long and slowly they formed in a big circle around one animal.

Matt reached for the telescope he always carried in his bag, balanced it on a flat rock and watched. The whale in the middle was lying very still. Suddenly the huge creature rolled and the others closed in an even tighter circle. *What is going on?* Matt wondered.

An hour passed. The whales were hardly moving. Then the tight ring broke as two whales dived. The whale in the centre rolled over once more and Matt saw the whales which had dived nudging something to the surface. It was a newborn baby, twelve-foot long. The ring was a protective circle. They were lifting the baby to the surface so it could take its first gulp of air.

The mother gently held her baby near the surface and each gasping breath sent a small plume of vapour into the sky. The pod of females once more formed the ring but this time their heads faced away from the centre.

There was danger! A group of killer whales had arrived. The killers, almost as large as the sperm whales, swam rapidly forward, bobbing their blunt heads high in the air to watch their quarry. They circled steadily, looking for a break. One swam towards a gap, but the menacing jaws of the sperm whales drove it back.

The baby, unaware of danger, swam towards its mother's tail. Two slits on each side of her belly held the nipples. It seized one. The mother, feeling her baby's urgent tug, squirted milk into the eager mouth.

The battle went on. Time after time the killers charged, and were beaten back by the alert females. Yet they were tiring. When still more killers arrived, the battle appeared lost.

Suddenly, bursting from the deep, rose the bull. Forty tons of furious weight, sixty-foot long, he reared high out of the water and fell with a splash that covered females, baby and killers in a layer of foam. Matt heard the bull's deep breathing out as an explosion that echoed over the water.

He had been lying three thousand feet below the surface, immobile, waiting for a giant squid to swim near his fearsome jaws. From the ocean surface had come the alarm calls of the females. With a powerful thrust of his great tail he shot his bulk towards the surface to do battle with the enemy above.

His first leap showed him the ring of killers. He seized the leader in a death grip, and tossed his victim high into the air. He charged again, using his huge head as a battering ram, sweeping the killer whales out of his majestic way. The rest broke in panic.

The danger was over. The bull and some of the females began to dive for food, yet some still stood guard over the mother and her baby.

Matt lay trembling with excitement. *What a sight! I bet there're not many people in the whole world who've seen such a battle. I bet they haven't*, he exulted. As he watched, the whales moved out into the open sea and disappeared in the mist.

He came down to earth. It was time to take a good look at that grey lump and then get back to the hut. Matt tipped the mass onto the ground.

It looks a bit like tallow, he thought, *but it doesn't smell like tallow. It's heavy, too.* He pressed his finger into the material then broke off a small piece.

Like a lump of cow dung, he decided in disgust but he was still puzzled. After all, sperm whales fed offshore and ambergris came from these whales.

During the next few days, using the axe, he broke the lump into pieces he could carry. He decided not to bring these to the hut. The sealers would know what ambergris was and it would be better to hide it some-where safe. The boys had found a cave deep in the bush so Matt shifted all the pieces to this cache, where it would be dry and hidden, covered with a layer of soil.

Perhaps it is ambergris, he said to himself. *That would be my first bit of good luck. Then there was the battle of the giants, my second bit of good luck. Dad always said good luck came in threes. I wonder what the next will be? Perhaps it will be Tom coming back.*

On the fifth day after Tom left, he walked along the coast to search the ruins of the old settlement where finding the whaler's gold might be his third bit of luck. Turning towards the ruins he saw a rock wallaby standing at the entrance to its rock shelter. Its fur shone golden in the sunlight. The animal took no notice of Matt but kept on grooming its fur, then it licked out its pouch and licked all over its forearms. Eyes fixed on the wallaby, Matt caught his foot in a creeper and came crashing to the ground. The wallaby heard, then saw him and bounded away over the rocks, sure-footed on its non-skid feet. Matt pushed his way through a yellow-green tangle of dodder laurel. Angrily he threw himself at the bundle of stems until more tough strands tripped him.

He pulled at the creeper and found he had uncovered the broken walls of a whaler's hut. This was one they had not found before, since it was well away from the edge of the main camp.

Excited now, Matt weeded the line of the walls until at last he had all the ruins in the open. He and Tom had often wondered where a person would hide treasure. They decided it would always be kept in or near the hut so if a whaler had to leave in a hurry he could get his coins, bundle them into his swag and take off. There was one place in a hut which was fairly safe, under the fire in the fireplace. When a man was in camp the fire never went out, so more coins could be added just by scraping away the coals, then digging up the tin the money was stored in.

Matt began to dig in the old hearth coated with ash. He had only a sharp stick and his knife so it was slow work. Just as he was ready to give up, the stick struck something hard. He dug deeper and his hands came to stone.

Disappointment.

Still he kept digging until it was uncovered. It was a single piece. Quickly he scraped around the edge then used the stick as a lever. The stone came away easily. Underneath was an iron pot. The lid was rusted and it took savage work with his knife to lever it away.

Matt saw a glint of yellow. Sovereigns, dozens, hundreds! He almost fainted with excitement. He spilled the coins on the ground and began counting. Two hundred and fifty-seven. It was a fortune! At the bottom of the pot he found the old whaler's well-thumbed Bible. It fell open at a spot where Matt read *the love of money is the root of all evil*.

I wonder if reading the Bible saved the old man from spending his money on drink and gambling? mused Matt. *Or if he had dreamed of going home to England.*

With the ambergris, if it was ambergris, and the sovereigns, which were real, he and Tom would be rich. Home Island had given them the start they needed, and with luck they could return to Albany and buy a small farm.

I must tell Tom, he resolved, *but first find a hiding place for the money.*

He spent the rest of the day looking for a spot well away from the ambergris. Tom might remember the cave and tell the sealers. If they found that, he was determined they at least wouldn't find the money.

Next morning he checked the few snares still set, and

skinned the catch, using the meat to make more stew. The sealers would soon be back. He thought how he could get Tom to leave the sealers without their finding out about the money and ambergris. They had taken the small sailboat so there was no way he could leave the island. What if he went with the sealers? No, he could never do that. He must hide and stay on the island. Then if any other ship came and the people looked honest he might be able to get help from friends in Albany. But no one must ever learn about the ambergris and the whaler's money. That would be his secret. It would be so easy to get rid of two boys and steal their treasure.

Finally he decided to play for time. He would leave a note in the hut so when the sealers came with Tom it would seem as though he still had not made up his mind but he would some time in the future, particularly if they left Tom behind to try and convince him.

Could he leave a clue about the treasure trove for Tom? No, he decided. It was too risky. Tom was not quick and when drunk on rum would be sure to blurt out the truth, boasting about what he would have one day. Matt wrote his note and waited, keeping a watchful eye on the sea to the east.

Three weeks after they had left the sealers returned. In the tea-tree scrub Matt watched them come to the hut, call to him, then stretch out on the ground while Tom cooked a meal. Tom and Bill climbed the small mountain, Tom's Peak, to search and shout but Matt stayed hidden, ready to take to his heels if they saw him.

The day passed slowly until, at last, the men walked to the beach and rowed to the ship. Soon it was sailing out of Home Bay, Tom still on board. Matt hurried to the hut. On the table was a note.

Dear Matt,
I am well. It's great fun on Seal Island. Bill says I will
become as good a sealer as enny of them. But we are all
leaving for Kangaroo Island soon. It is right across the
Big Bite and we mite never come back. We will come
back in a month and that will be your last chance.
Please join us Matt. I am lonely without you and
worried you may be sick. Be waiting when I come back.
Tom

If I'd read that while they were still here, thought Matt,
I might have gone with Tom.

chapter ten

A STRANGER

The days passed slowly. Matt wondered what Tom was doing, but always in his mind was the excitement of THE TREASURE. He thought of it in capital letters, always.

In the second week after Tom's visit to the island, a small sailing boat approached from the west, cautiously, as though the steersman did not know the coast. Matt watched through the telescope as the man leaned over the side, carefully studying the water depth. He seemed to be the only person on board, so Matt decided to take a risk and ran along the beach pointing to the channel that led to a good anchorage close in.

The man waved in greeting, anchored his boat and dived straight overboard. It seemed he couldn't wait to put the dinghy in the water. Powerful strokes brought him quickly to shallow water where he could wade ashore.

Tall, brown from sun and air, he was not exactly

ragged but he did not look prosperous. He was impressively bearded and through long hair his eyes twinkled at Matt.

'Hello there, lad. And are you king of this island or is it crown prince, with your dad as king?'

Matt laughed, for the man's smile was infectious. 'I don't know about kings and princes but I'm ...' he broke off.

If the man was dangerous it would be better to leave the impression that his father was nearby and might be back later, or that he had others in the bush who would soon be back ready to protect him.

The man looked at him sharply. 'Ah lad, I see you're wise. Best be careful. Bad cess to me that I didn't learn that lesson back home in Ireland. Well my boy, I'm Michael. Perhaps you've heard of me? And I think you must be young Somers. Matthew is it? Or Tom?'

Hope surged.

'You know my dad? When did you see him last?'

'A year ago. He was to pick me up along the coast from Albany. I was running late and missed him, but some other friends helped me. Somers told me he was making a home somewhere on the islands, taking his two boys. I'm looking forward to seeing him again and meeting his sons.'

'You're Michael, the Fenian!' cried Matt, as he remembered the long wait near the shore, and his father's story about the Irish patriot.

Matt sat on the sand and gestured to Michael to do the same. He poured out the story of their life on the island, the long wait for their father, their worry, and last, the arrival of the sealers and their news that their father had drowned and the *Silver Gull* wrecked somewhere to the west. Then he burst into tears.

Michael consoled the sobbing boy, enfolding him in a great bear hug. Gradually his tears dried. His father had never been much for hugging or for words of praise. He wanted them to grow up tough, but here was a man who seemed a mix of his father and mother. Tough as jarrah but with warmth. Matt would never have thought of hugging his own father.

'That story came from the sealers. Perhaps they lied to you so you'd go with them.'

Matt was thunderstruck. He had never thought of that. Hope surged once more. Perhaps his father was alive. Then hope plunged again. He was sure old Sam had told the truth and Bill, tough sealer though he was, had a rough honesty. And why hadn't Dad come? He wouldn't have waited so long, not Dad.

Michael watched the expressions of hope, then misery, flit across the boy's face. He would never make a poker player, that boy. It was the kind of face he liked. Not like those who hid their feelings behind a mask. You couldn't tell if they were your mate or ready to sell you to the police for the reward.

'Ah lad, best fear the worst yet hope for the best. I must say I can't see Somers leaving you alone for nearly a year. He was a hard man but not that hard. I did hear of a wreck along the coast but didn't know it was your dad.'

'We waited a week for you. Dad thought a lot of you. Said you were a hero, even though wrong-headed.'

'True enough,' said Michael ruefully. 'Wrong-headed, but not stupid enough to let the police catch me. If they ever do, it'll be when I'm dead. I'll never be a convict again. Come now, Matthew — it's a grand name, Matthew. A good name for an English boy.'

'Australian,' said Matt sternly. 'Dad told us we're

finished with England. Australia is our home and the sooner we think of this land as home the better for all of us.'

'A good man, your dad. Given time I might have made him understand why Ireland must be free. We all need roots, and in time you'll find this country is just as beautiful, just as interesting as any place in Europe.'

'I don't need time,' replied Matt sturdily. 'I know it now.'

'Let's be up and be going to your hut where I can have a drink of tea and a bite of food, for I need to dry off outside as much as I need a wet inside me.'

They were soon at the hut and Michael walked over to the pot simmering over the fire, pushed in a fork and pulled out a steaming potato.

'There you have it, Matt. The blessing and the curse of old Ireland.'

'A potato?' exclaimed Matt.

'Yes, the humble tatie. It was a curse and a blessing to our old green home.'

'But what's wrong with them?' persisted Matt. 'I love them. I eat them every day and never get tired of them.'

'Ah lad, that's the curse of the tatie. It seemed like a blessing. Easy to grow, easy to hide when the tax collector came and there was no need to work for a master when you had a bit of land to grow the potato. "Another baby in the cot, another tatie in the pot" was my mother's old saying.'

'What's wrong with that?' argued Matt.

'Nothing. Nothing at all until the blight came. It was terrible! A disease which came from England, and how it got there I don't know. It swept the country like a fire and the potato crops failed. Every tatie rotted in the ground. There were four million Irish people when it

99

came in 1845. A year later a quarter of them were dead. Men, women and children starved or died from disease. And the English did little. As for the landlords they had other food, but the peasants, the people, had nothing.'

'A million people!' exclaimed Matt. 'The English should have done better.'

'All my family died. A million fled the country. Most to America. It's a country I want to get to. They've always been good friends to the Irish. But enough of my troubles. Now it's your turn. Where is your brother?'

It was a bursting of the floodgates. Matt poured out the rest of the story of their life on the island, their near poisoning with brackish water, old Sam the sealer and the rest of his band. The seal hunt and their enticing Tom to go with them to their base on Seal Island to the east. He took Tom's notes from the cupboard and showed them to Michael. Then he decided to tell Michael the secret of the treasure. Luck maybe went in fours instead of threes. The coming of the Fenian may have been the best of all. He needed a strong man to help him in the fight to save Tom.

Michael pursed his lips in a soundless whistle. 'Well, Matthew my boy, you've certainly had your adventures. You are a surprise. Here I thought you were a poor wee boy and I find you're a lad of substance. Later I'll look at that ambergris of yours just to make sure it's not tallow or grease or whale blubber, but it sounds good.'

'Now ... about Tom.' He thought for a while. Matt waited, eyes alight with new hope.

'Right. Let me get this clear. How many hours' sail to Seal Island?'

'With a good wind, about six, the sealers said.'

'That means we could run our easting down during the night and with luck be hidden in some bay before the sealers are awake.'

'You think we can get to Tom?'

'We can but try. The hard thing will be to get the lad on his own so we can talk to him, persuade him to leave with us, without the sealers knowing. All in all, I'd rather the sealers didn't see me, or you! We might have to lie hidden all day. Spot will have to stay on the boat. Can't have him barking our whereabouts.'

'We can leave him on Home Island.'

'We can't come back here. You'll have to let Podge go back to the sea too. If we did come back the sealers would be on us in a few days. We'll go east.'

'East!' cried Matt in horror. 'Across the Bight? In that tiny boat? We'll never make it.'

'She's a good boat,' said Michael defensively. 'I've spent more of my life on boats than I care to remember. Boats big and small. I built this one and I tell you I could take it around the world, given time. The roaring forties will push us along, and no sealer will catch us. Not in their great, round-bottomed tubs, fit only for carrying sealskins and oil. Not that they aren't good boats of their kind,' he admitted, 'but not fast. Not like my little beauty, which I named *the Wild Goose*. She'll fly in the wind.'

'I know why you called it that,' exclaimed Matt. 'Dad told us about the newspaper on the convict ship.'

Michael nodded. 'There are hundreds of islands just like this off the South Australian coast. And there's the mainland. You could start a farm if you wanted.'

'But what would happen to us when we reached South Australia?'

Michael stroked his beard, then said, 'I'll give it some

thought. Somewhere back in England you'll have relatives — all keen to look after you and also, of course, your money. You'd be lucky to see any of it when you're twenty-one and free to do what you like.'

'Six years,' worried Matt, 'before Tom will be old enough and he won't listen to me.'

'You've two choices. You can tell me to push off and I'll leave you after getting some wallaby meat, damper and fresh water. Then you'll be back in your old position. I don't know where your ambergris is or your money.'

'No,' cried Matt in horror. 'No. Don't leave.'

'Thank you, Matt. The second choice is that I can take the place of your father. Though it may not be according to law I'll be a father to you both.'

'Of course,' agreed Matt, 'and I'm sure when Tom gets to know you, he'll say the same.'

'Good. Then we could use your money to buy a snug little farm, perhaps in the Adelaide hills. You can stay there and work it, or we could get in a manager, get ourselves a nice outfit and head for the diggings. They tell me you can pick up gold in any creek in Victoria and New South Wales. Even if we didn't find much gold, we'd enjoy ourselves, I warrant. When you're old enough to go your own way, I'd say goodbye and head for America. What do you say? Are you with me?'

'Yes.'

'Life is a chancy thing,' Michael paused. 'I'll draw up a will, with a lawyer, so the farm will be given to you and Tom if I die or as soon as you are twenty-one. And we can also have a deed which says the money is all yours — sovereigns and ambergris alike — and that you are letting me be the trustee until you are twenty-one. That means nobody, not even me, can take it from you.

'Tell me about Seal Island,' Michael continued.

'It runs north and south with the best anchorage at the northern end. That's where the main harbour is. Sam told us that. On the east coast there are beaches but not much shelter if the wind backs round.'

'So,' said Michael, 'if we ran around the south end and coasted along in the early morning, keeping to the eastern shore, we would be hidden from the sealers' camp.'

'Unless some of them were wandering along the ridge,' cautioned Matt.

'Hardly likely if they're sealers. They're a lazy lot. Much more likely to be lying around the camp and keeping Tom busy feeding them. They've got to get the cargo ready for the run to Kangaroo Island too. That all sounds hopeful. Let's hope they don't decide to take a walk for the good of their health. Ah well,' he concluded, 'what's life without a bit of risk?'

'Now for stores. We'll need to take as much damper as you can bake. It won't last long but what's a bit of mould when you're hungry? And taties. Boiled taties will keep, and we can take as many sacks as we can of fresh ones. And flour, as well as any other stores we're going to need.'

'I thought you wouldn't eat taties after what they did to Ireland,' suggested Matt with a grin.

'Don't be cheeky, boy,' Michael gave him a playful punch. 'We'll also need hard-boiled eggs, and plenty of meat.'

'It'll go bad,' objected Matt.

'We can dry fresh meat in the sun and smoke it from a fire so it stays dry. Later you can cook it in a stew and very good it is. Or you can chew it. Tough as boot leather but tasty. We'll catch some wallabies and dry

103

the meat in the sun. In this weather it should be done in a few days.

'We'll need to load your skins and get the ambergris and sovereigns on the boat. Must find a way to make the ambergris look like skins, and the sovereigns we can bury in the stores, maybe in the flour.'

It was settled. They started to dry the meat and packed the skins into the boat. They collected the money and went to the cave to get the ambergris.

Back in the hut Michael put a needle in the fire and when the end was glowing, pricked the grey mass.

'You see, lad, fat or grease will just melt. Ambergris will bubble from the needle and stick to your fingers. Just like that. By God, it is ambergris!' He smelled the material. 'There's a fortune in the lump. Not hundreds like your sovereigns, but thousands if I can sell it in the right market.' He thought for a moment. 'I may have to go to Sydney, or London even, but it would be worth it.'

The work continued but now with great hopes. Their future was safe if they could only get Tom to come with them, and get to Adelaide. They put fresh water in the casks, cooked potatoes, and dug up fresh ones as well as other vegetables. They stacked the stores still left from the *Silver Gull* in the hold of the boat. If they made a landfall on the thousands of miles across the Bight it would be easy to light a fire and cook more food. They had lines to catch fish. They ate some of the fowls and Matt let the rest go.

They tested the rigging and took what they had in the hut to repair any that had frayed. There were long lines of cliffs along the Great Australian Bight and landing would not be easy.

A fortnight later all was ready. 'Well, lad,' agreed

Michael, 'I can't think of anything else to do so I declare tomorrow a holiday. We can say goodbye properly to Home Island, and in the afternoon we'll leave.'

'Great,' agreed Matt. 'I'll take you to say goodbye to the dolphins.'

The Irishman looked sceptical but he made no comment. Next morning on the beach with Spot and Podge, both wildly excited, Matt beat on the water with a stick. Soon a pair of dolphins came sweeping inshore. Matt swam out with fish they had caught the night before and gave them to the dolphins. For a time boy and dolphins frolicked, then Matt swam back. Michael met him on the shore, his mouth falling open in amazement.

'Well I've been in most parts of the world but I've never seen anything like that. You're a magician, lad. Is it King Solomon's Ring you be having?'

'King Solomon's Ring?' asked Matt, puzzled.

'Yes, me boy. It was said that King Solomon had a ring and when he wore it he could talk to the animals just like you did calling those dolphins to the shore. I remember reading how dolphins became friendly with humans two thousand years ago in the Mediterranean. And Black Ted claimed that in Queensland his tribe used dolphins to help them catch fish. Why didn't you train your pets to do the same?'

'It was the other way round,' explained Matt. 'We gave them fish and that's why they came. Cupboard love really, but it was great fun and I think they did like playing with us because even after we ran out of fish the dolphins stayed with us for hours.'

'It beats everything,' said Michael. 'I can see why you love this island.'

Matt hid his shells and the rest of his collection in the cave where they should be safe until he and Tom returned. He vowed that they would return one day. What memories he had!

In the late afternoon they were ready. They pulled the dinghy on board. Podge was in the water.

'Goodbye, Podge. Goodbye.'

They set sail and soon, with the freshening wind, left Podge far behind as they headed for the open sea.

Matt thought of the year he and Tom had enjoyed on this island. The climb to Tom's Peak and the magic day when the dolphins formed the great circle near Goose Island.

'Look Matt,' cried Michael. 'Your friends have come to say goodbye.' Rolling towards them in joyful exuberance, a pair of dolphins, their bodies golden in the setting sun, swam towards them and took a place at the bow. More arrived to swim around the boat, before leaving as mysteriously as they had come.

'It's a good omen,' declared Michael. 'The sea goddess has wished us luck. The dolphins are her hand-maidens and we couldn't have a luckier send-off.'

Matt was silent. Tomorrow they would succeed or fail. They needed all the blessings of any sea spirits there were. At least they could say they had tried.

He looked back at the island framed in the setting sun as it sank blood red into the sea. Whatever happened there was one golden year to remember.

chapter eleven

SEAL ISLAND

Through the night they sailed, with the breeze steady and strong. Both were silent, each occupied with their own thoughts.

Perhaps I can forget the dream of a new Ireland in America and make this southland my home, mused Michael. *Now I've met this lively lad and soon will meet his brother, life may get a new purpose. Perhaps these are the sons I thought I would never have.*

Will Tom have changed? wondered Matt. *Will life among the sealers have sickened him and will he now be ready to leave? I'm sure once he meets Michael and talks to him and I tell him about the treasure he'll want to come with us.*

The moon rose and Matt scrambled up the mast like a monkey. He was searching for the loom of land which would show Seal Island was near. Suddenly he saw it, a dark mass on the horizon. Michael moved quickly to drop the mainsail which shone like a beacon in the moonlight. The boat slowed, driven only by the jib. In

107

this dim light he doubted if any sealer could catch a glimpse of their boat. All would be fast asleep after the day's work preparing to leave the island. Then cloud covered the moon and he pulled up the mainsail once more to make as much distance as they could before dawn. Now they were heading towards the island's southernmost tip.

The sea broke on awesome cliffs here and they kept well offshore. Seals lay on the rocks, safe where even the most venturesome of sealers would not dare land. Soon they were able to head north once more, now in the lee of the land, protected from the roaring forties, the westerlies which ran their steady course around the globe. It was not only more comfortable but faster, with no huge swells to slow their progress. They had to reach near the northern end before they searched for an anchorage, otherwise they would have too long a walk to the sealers' camp.

'I think with their planned shift to Kangaroo Island, they'll be too busy to wander along this eastern coast,' Michael told Matt. 'All the sealskins will have to be packed and the oil stowed. They will need to kill walla-bies to dry and do all the hundred and one things needed before shifting a main camp like this. They'll never return to this Recherche Archipelago because most of the seals are finished. They'll need to search for new killing fields. And each man will have to collect and hide his money.'

'Would they have much?' wondered Matt.

'Ah yes. There's the stuff they sell to whaling ships and each man would have his share from selling skins, oil and fresh meat. Then they gamble – or most do. I've known some to win so much that the others killed them in rage and envy before they could even get back on board. The owner of the sovereigns you found was lucky he was able to hide them safely. In a sealing gang you get some of the worst.'

'And some of the best,' replied Matt. 'I'm sure old Sam was an honest man. I'd trust him.'

'Yes. Some of the best as well. I heard of a chap named Munro who was known as the King of the Straitsmen. Bass Strait that was. He ruled his kingdom among the Eastern Straitsmen. On Kangaroo Island they have the Western Straitsmen but I don't know who rules the roost there. Whoever it is, we'll keep away from that group and head for Adelaide.'

Michael continued, 'It's lucky the sealers are making a big move. Perhaps that will make them careless. They'll know Tom will not want to be marooned on Seal Island, so he'll be safe enough for a few days 'til they sail to Home Island, where they hope to pick up another likely lad. If they can't find you, they'll head east again and think you're no great loss.'

'Look sharp. It's getting lighter. Watch for a good anchorage.'

Steadily they moved along the coast until Matt pointed, 'What about that spot behind the small island?'

'Just the ticket,' agreed Michael. It was a tiny bay and the island lay in its arms. It had an offshore reef to provide a snug shelter where the boat could lie safe, while the island would hide it from view. It was only a few hundred yards to shore. Soon they were in the bay and heading for the anchorage. A cloud of birds rose in alarm as they dropped anchor. Matt worried they might give their presence away to the sealers.

'No,' encouraged Michael. 'Those are divers. Terns,

people call them. Nesting, I'll be bound, and they often rise in dreads like that. They'll forget us soon and go on with their nesting unless we land on their island. Must be about five hundred, and a few gulls ready to steal eggs and chicks. Great nest robbers gulls be, and not my favourite birds.'

'The divers are as big as the gulls and should be able to drive them away,' suggested Matt. 'Still they are bossy birds. Look, Michael, gannets.'

A dozen silvery birds much bigger than gulls or divers rose and circled before flying further out to sea where they plunged into the water like feathered spears. The divers and gulls followed and soon there was a flurry of splashes showing where all had plunged.

'Are we going ashore now?' asked Matt.

'No, too risky. A man walking alone might be mistaken for another sealer. A boy would give the game away. We'll just get some sleep. In the late afternoon we'll walk along the beach to the north, then climb to the top of the ridge so we can watch the camp. I'll take the telescope so we can see what's happening and how close the sealers are to leaving.'

'What will we do if they see us?' asked Matt.

'Run. Run like crazy, boy. As though your life depended on it. They don't know where our boat is, so if we reach it first, we put to sea.'

'But that means we leave Tom,' cried Matt.

'I'm afraid so. The sealers will think we're heading back to Home Island and they'll forget us. Once they know you have a friend with a boat they'll know you're safe and won't go with them, but our chance of getting Tom has gone. But cheer up. They're heading for Kangaroo Island and Tom can't come to any real harm on the boat. We can be waiting on Kangaroo Island where they won't be expecting us and then we'll see. If I can't rescue him then, my name's not Michael.' He continued, 'We should take enough food and water for at least tonight and tomorrow. We might have to stay in hiding all tomorrow as well. Tom might wander to the top of the ridge where we'll be hiding and that would make it easy. But we may have to wait another day so we must have plenty of water at least. Food we can do without at a pinch, but in this sun, without water, we'd be in trouble.'

They took warm clothes and strong boots, choosing dull garments, hard to see against the rocks and shrubs. Wrapping everything in canvas they held these bundles on their heads and swam for the shore, using a side-stroke with one arm so their heads would remain above water. They tied their boots around their necks. On the beach they pulled on clothes but stayed barefoot, as the longest walk would be on sand. This was easy going. When they at last reached a rock barrier they pulled on their boots to climb up the rocky slope to the base of the ridge. By this time the sun had set but a rising moon made walking easy. Michael pulled out his watch and studied it.

'We must be about level with the camp. If I haven't made a mistake we can head for that high ground. Try not to disturb too many rock wallabies. We'll have to be careful not to stumble and send too many rocks rolling down the slope. A few won't matter as the sealers will be used to wallabies making a lot of clatter, but if they catch a sight of us, it'll be too bad.'

Silently they made their way to the top of the limestone ridge that ran along the spine of Seal Island. It was here that the wallabies sheltered in the shade during the day, coming out at night to feed. Half an hour's walking brought them to the top, and in the distance they could see the twinkle of a fire near the beach. They then searched for a sheltered spot where they could sleep for the rest of the night yet remain hidden by day. They found a perfect place, a large overhang with a sandy floor and, even better, a slab of rock which had tumbled from the roof to form a natural wall with a few cracks. They could look through these at the sealers' camp, yet remain hidden.

There was no more to do. They stretched out on the sandy floor and, lulled by the distant murmur of the waves breaking on the beach and tired from the long day, fell asleep.

Matt woke first. It was early morning. For a few seconds he stared at the white roof of the cave, unsure where he was, then it all came to him. They were near the enemy camp and he had better be careful how he moved. Creeping to the sheltering rock he peered through the cracks at the sealers' camp. Men were gathered around the camp fire. Most were puffing at clay pipes while a few were staring at the big, black pot steaming on the fire.

Matt went back for the telescope and lifted it gently into position, careful that the glass was in the shade so it would not send a warning reflection towards the camp. However the sun was rising on the east side while the sealers' camp, being on the north, was still partly in shade. He adjusted the focus and the white dots sharpened to recognisable faces. There was Bill staring into the fire. Next to him was old Sam puffing at a pipe. Matt felt pleased. He was sure that if the worst came to the worst he would have a friend in Sam. But where was Tom?

One of the sealers walked over to a heap of blankets

and kicked it aside. He pulled on a rope as though dragging a dog and Tom stumbled to his feet. Tom! Tethered like an animal! He laid down the telescope and ran to Michael, tugging on his sleeve. It was terrifying to see how quickly the Irishman came alert, like a tiger ready to spring.

I am glad he's on our side, thought Matt, for the hundredth time.

He told him what he'd seen, with a catch in his voice. Michael laughed softly.

'I guess Tom got sick of working in the camp and ran to the south end. They'd have had a lot of trouble bringing him back so they decided it was better to tie him at night so he'd be ready to get breakfast in the morning. It's good though. It shows Tom has kept his spirit, as I'd expect from a Somers lad. And he'll want to come with us. Let's have a look.'

A plate of stew had been pushed into Tom's bound hands and he was eating hungrily.

'At least he's not sick,' sighed Matt. 'Look how he's wolfing down that food.'

Michael scanned the camp. He studied the beach, the ship and the stores. Then he looked up the hill. There was a path from the camp straight up the slope and it came very close to where they were hidden. Another fainter path ran to the south.

'Do you see the track running from here to the camp?'

Matt nodded.

'Tonight we can reach the camp using that without making too much noise, or sending rocks down the hill. That solves our biggest problem. There seems to be at least a day's work loading the ship. I can't be sure though. It looks like a long day for us, just sitting here and waiting. It would be suicide to try anything until after dark. When you've been in as many battles as I have, you'll learn that most of your time is spent waiting.'

'What about Tom?' Matt asked, worrying about that rope.

'Bear up, lad. I guess it will be taken off now they can keep an eye on him. They're going to need him for cooking and helping load the ship. See! They're untying him now.'

Tom was moving freely, went over to the fire and came back with another heaped plateful.

'Nothing wrong with his appetite,' laughed Michael.

The hours passed slowly. The cave became warmer as the sun swung high. Michael made Matt sip their water slowly.

'We'll have to keep most of it for tonight and perhaps tomorrow. A long walk back to the boat to get more.'

'Another day,' cried Matt. 'I couldn't stand it.'

'You'll have to. Remember those who travel in haste repent at leisure.'

'You've got a saying for everything, Michael,' objected Matt in exasperation.

'Now listen carefully. This is my plan. When it's dark we'll creep down to the camp. Your job will be to cut the rope that's holding your brother, as soon as you get the chance. Put a hand over his mouth so he won't call out. Keep the knife in your hand just in case.'

'In case of what?' Matt exclaimed in horror.

'We aren't playing games. We're dealing with dangerous men who'll cut your throat if it suits them. If Tom can get hold of a club all the better. If anyone tries to stop you, swing the knife. You won't need to actually stab anyone but it might make them stop for a minute.

You must run like the wind. Both Tom and you should be able to run faster than any sealer. Got that? Wait your chance and cut the rope. Then run.'

'Yes,' said Matt.

'Repeat it,' ordered Michael.

Satisfied that Matt knew what to do he went on. 'The sealers may think you're running to the beach so that should give you more time. Wait for me at this cave and eat some food and drink some water. Leave enough for me. If I don't come and you see the sealers beginning to move up this path — you'll see their torches a long way off — get moving back to the boat.'

'But what will you do?' asked Matt anxiously.

'If I haven't come, it's because I've been killed, injured or captured. Then it will all be up to you. Once on the boat, wait as long as you can. If you see the sealers coming towards the bay, up anchor and keep sailing east. Do the best you can. She's a good boat and I bet Tom knows his way around the sea. We might meet again in South Australia, but the best of luck.' He gripped Matt's shoulder firmly.

'It's in God's hands now. All I'm going to do is to give him a helping shove along.'

Matt knew his dry mouth was from fear, not thirst.

'Be brave, boy. Tom's safety depends on your keeping a cool head.' Michael went on with his instructions. 'Remember I may change plans in midstream through what we hear. If I do, just watch for your chance to go to Tom, cut the rope and take to your heels. Be as quiet as death itself. Noise can spoil it all.'

As the hours passed they watched the sealers carrying the stores to the ship. The pile became smaller and smaller and it seemed as though all would be finished by nightfall with departure in the morning. Tonight was the night.

'Right,' said Michael when the sun had set and a faint sky light allowed them to see the bigger stones that lay in their path. 'Later there'll be a moon which will help you on the run. Get moving my boy.'

They clambered over the rocks to the path and hid the remaining food and water. It was easy to see even without light. At this time of the year the sky never became entirely dark, except on a cloudy night. Tonight the sky was clear, star-bright. They moved quietly towards the camp until they could hear voices and even catch occasional words. Michael gestured towards a heap of stones which would provide a hiding place. Deep in its shadow they lay waiting. Then they heard the captain. 'We've done a good job today. Tomorrow we'll cast off.'

'Are we going to pick up the other boy?'

Matt recognised the voice of Weaselface.

'Of course,' said the skipper. 'We can do with two bright lads.'

'Once we've tamed them,' chuckled Weaselface. 'Young Tom is still a bit sullen, aren't you boy?' and he tugged on the rope causing Tom to stumble and fall forward.

'Enough of that,' growled Bill. 'I'll have no hurting the lad. Come on, Tom. Sit near the fire and get a tot of rum in you. We'll need to make an early start for the run to Home Island. Always tough reaching into the wind, unless we get a change during the night. But it doesn't look as though we will.' He stared into the western sky.

'We can all do with a drink. Pass up that rum jar, Sam.'

The jar passed rapidly from hand to hand. Gradually

the men's voices rose as they told each other stories, most already heard a hundred times. Stories of right whales caught, of oil casks brimming, of lumps of ambergris bigger than a man's head, of sealskins soft as a woman's skin. As the rum moved fast, so too did the stories. They began to boast of raids on Aboriginal camps. How they killed the men and took the women and young girls. Of gambling nights when all the money was lost and the gamblers began using women as tokens, passing them over as casually as sealskins to be traded.

Suddenly Tom's captor broke in. 'Stories are stories. I want action. There's Tom here. He hasn't been initiated yet. Won't be a good sealer until he has.'

A chorus of approval greeted his remark. 'Me first,' cried another. Tom dragged himself away from the fire as far as the rope would allow.

Matt started to his feet but was pulled down by a powerful hand, while a rough palm clamped on his mouth.

'Do you want to get us killed?' whispered Michael. 'Don't be a fool. Or do you want to make it two boys instead of only one for them to play with?'

Matt shuddered but was stilled by the good sense of those words. 'We must do something,' he whispered.

'We will, but no rushing like a bull at a gate. I've a plan. When the time comes and all the men are looking at me, you slip quietly along and cut the rope. Then away to the path and wait near the food and water. Be quiet now and listen.'

An argument had broken out around the fire. Old Sam was trying to rescue Tom from the sealer who held the rope, but a powerful punch sent him crashing to the ground.

The others laughed. 'Who would have thought old Sam was wanting first go at the boy,' one sealer cried. 'I thought he was too old for that sort of caper.'

'He may be old but he's frisky,' laughed another.

'Enough of that,' ordered Bill. 'We'll have no fighting over the lad.'

'What will we have then?' asked a tall sealer, 'because we're going to have the lad whether you like it or not.'

'Oh, will you?' growled Bill, striding to the speaker and smashing him to the ground with a blow which showed why he was the leader, the proud bull among all the males. 'Anyone else who wants to take my place?' and he glared around the group.

Even his bristles are standing stiff, marvelled Matt *and he is as big and tough as Michael.*

The men quietened but there was a steady undercurrent of grumbling. The captain looked around, satisfied now that he was once more in charge. But he knew how light a rein he must keep on the sealers.

'Right then. There's only one way to settle this. We'll draw lots. Longest straw gets the boy.'

There came a roar of approval and the rum jar went around even faster as one sealer gathered sticks which he broke into small, even pieces with only one long stick left among them. He shuffled these in a hairy paw, then held them out with only the even ends showing.

'Right boys. Line up and take your pick.'

The men crowded around and began to pull. There were cries of disappointment as the first comers drew short sticks.

Suddenly a rich Irish voice spoke from the darkness. 'You'll need another straw if I'm to take a hand.'

Michael stepped into the firelight. He looked huge in the flickering light. There was a clamour of voices and the captain bellowed for silence.

'Now mister, who may you be, dropping from the sky like that?'

'Sure, I'm Michael. Michael O'Dwyer, a name you may have heard, if you've been on the west coast or in old Ireland.'

'Michael O'Dwyer,' cried one of the sealers. 'Not the Fenian, the man who led the rising in County Clare?'

'The same,' replied Michael quietly.

'God bless us,' cried the speaker as he rushed forward and enfolded Michael in gorilla-like arms. 'Ah me broth of a boy, I only wish I'd been with you on that glorious day. Sure haven't I told them a hundred times how you stole the muskets under the noses of the police, bad cess to them. And took to the hills. They would never have caught you if it hadn't been for that English spy, may he rot in hell. They make songs about you.'

'But it was an Irishman who took the bribe to say where I was hiding,' said Michael drily. 'There be traitors in Ireland too.'

The men murmured in excitement. A third of them were Irish, most were convicts sent to Australia for stealing in England or rebelling in Ireland. All hated and feared authority, and here was a hero who had become a legend. A wave of goodwill towards the tall Irishman swept the group. They all wanted to shake his hand. The captain was the last.

'How did you get here then?' he asked.

'Ah, I had a bit of luck in the west and decided to take my chance at the diggings in the east. They tell me there's some big finds. I built a small boat and ran east hoping to reach Kangaroo Island, then on to the diggings. Better to pick up gold from the ground than

119

make a poor living and a dangerous one chasing whales and clubbing seals. I saw your fire and decided to anchor offshore and see who you were, though I'd been told in Albany there were sealers on this coast.'

The skipper's face cleared. 'You're welcome then and we'll talk more about the goldfields. They tell me there's been a big find in New South Wales.'

'Yes,' interjected another. 'I heard you can pick up nuggets in the creeks near Bathurst and Gulgong.'

'Too close to the police for my liking,' complained a sealer. 'At least we're safe from the traps out here. No soldiers coming this far either.'

As soon as Matt saw Michael had captured the attention of the sealers, he crept forward, held his hand over Tom's mouth then cut the rope binding his hands. Both began to crawl from the circle of firelight and, once on the path, took to their heels, running up the hill. When they reached the water and food both ate and drank fast, then sat and watched the distant camp fire. Tom listened in astonishment as Matt told him of his adventures and of Michael and the treasure. When Matt spoke of the boat and how they were to sail to the east, his eyes began to glow.

'Wonderful, Matt. You're a bonzer kid. When do we head for the boat?'

'As soon as Michael gets here. He's still in danger.' They both turned towards the camp but could see nothing and hear nothing. Tom's comment about being a kid still rankled with Matt. Tom hadn't changed.

Michael had seen Tom's escape and took a deep breath. One problem gone and only one left. 'It's dry work talking. How about a tot of rum?'

'Sorry,' said the skipper. 'We just drained the jar.'

'Not to worry. I've a few bottles of square-faced gin in my boat. Better than rum I'd be thinking.'

'Gin's a woman's drink,' objected Weaselface, who was still holding the end of the rope.

'A woman's drink is it?' cried Michael 'And would you like to be showing me what a woman I am?'

The man shifted his feet uneasily. 'No offence, mate,' he said sullenly.

'And who said you were my mate?' asked Michael truculently. 'And what would you know about gin, holding a bit of rope like a zany.'

The sealer flushed and took a step forward as though to attack, then felt the lack of pull on the rope and turned to look. He swore in panic.

'God. That bloody boy's slung his hook. The rope's been cut.'

'A boy is it?' cried Michael. 'That'll be the lad who passed me on the way to the beach. Didn't say a word but kept running. I thought he was sent to see if the ship was all right.'

'He might cast the ship adrift,' roared the captain. 'Or take off himself, cut the anchor to try to sail back to Home Island. He's stupid enough for that. All of you after him. Whoever catches the rascal has him for the night.'

The men ran pell-mell for the beach with the captain in the lead. They were eager to catch Tom, but even more they dreaded what might happen if they lost the ship. They ran fast, shouting with fury. All except one man — Weaselface, who stood, still holding the rope end.

'You're not after the boy?' asked Michael.

'No,' he growled. 'I'm wondering how it was you came to our camp just as the boy found a knife from somewhere to cut the rope. What have you to say about that?' he finished angrily.

'Just this,' replied Michael as his massive fist shot out like a battering ram. All the anger and disgust he had felt while watching the sealers bartering for poor Tom, tied on the end of a rope, was in that punch. The man went down like a poleaxed bullock, his jaw broken.

'Wait for your mates,' jeered Michael and disappeared up the path, but the sealer was too hurt to follow. The Fenian did not pause until he reached the boys.

'Welcome to the crew, Tom. I bet Matt's told you the whole story. Let's get moving. They'll soon find there's no boat of mine and no sign of you. There's no square-faced gin either. If there had been I'd have drunk it long ago. Now, no more talking. Save your breath for running. Just show me how you can run faster than Matt.'

Tom needed no urging to lead the way along the track. Soon they were on the top of the ridge and, looking back, saw the torches wavering in the distance. Most were still on the beach but some were heading back to the camp where they would learn what had happened from Weaselface, providing he could make himself understood with his broken jaw.

An hour later they were on the beach. Barefoot now, they ran along the sand towards the bay where the boat was at anchor. The sea glittered in the moonlight, and the going was much easier so they made good time. At last they reached the bay, with the island dark on the water. The sea chill took away any tiredness and they clambered onto the boat. Tom raised the jib and mainsail without needing any instructions, while Michael and Matt hauled on the anchor rope. Soon they had the anchor firmly tied to the deck.

Then, with Michael at the tiller, the boat turned in the wind and began to make headway.

'A grand night's work,' shouted Michael. 'I haven't felt so good since that day in County Clare when I was a lad, not much older than yourself, Tom. Now you take the tiller. See that star to the east? It's the evening star, Venus. But you're too young to be caring for that grand lady. Steer for her Tom. She'll be as good a guide as any for the new life we're starting.'

The sail bellied, and the wind strengthened as they moved from the shelter of Seal Island. The boat lifted to the huge swells of the southern ocean, pushed by the roaring forties. A wandering albatross glided behind them, then moved effortlessly past downwind and disappeared in the darkness.

Tom held the tiller firm and stared forward, feet apart, alert for any change in the sails' trim. Michael watched him approvingly.

Matt saw the bulk of Seal Island fading astern with a glow of satisfaction. They had rescued Tom! What a future they had! His thoughts ranged over the year he and Tom had ruled their kingdom of Home Island. *We have both changed*, he thought. *But whatever happens now we'll never forget those days when we were just the Crusoe boys.*

AFTERWORD

In 1951 I was a zoologist with an Australian Geographical Society expedition to the Recherche Archipelago off the south coast of Western Australia. Our leader, John Bechervaise, a distinguished polar explorer, brought with him an account recently written by T C Andrews, who had lived on one of these islands as a boy. This valuable document is now in the archives of the Western Australian State Library.

At the age of 83, Andrews had set down recollections of his boyhood, for his family and their children. The world he described has survived to the modern day. The Recherche Archipelago is almost unchanged. It is a nature reserve, a piece of Australia saved for all time for the enjoyment of Australians today and in the future.

The journal tells of a time, more than a hundred years ago now, when Andrews and his brother lived for eight months on Middle Island, the largest of the group we explored. His father planned to settle on the island later in the year. He left the boys with strict instructions on the work they were to do while waiting for his return. It was a Robinson Crusoe type of existence, except the father's rules were to be the boys' guide.

'The best time of my whole life,' was how Andrews remembered those months on Middle Island. The story made such an impression on me that I have used it as a framework for this book.

As a child I lived on a farm, in conditions similar to those of the Andrews boys. I also studied seabirds for six months on a coral island in the Abrolhos Group, off the coast of Western Australia, and I have worked on many other islands around Australia. The natural history in these pages is a combination of Andrews' and my own experiences.

The adventures with nature are accurate, the adventures with other humans are fictitious. They are based on historical records of the nineteenth-century life of the whalers and sealers in the seas off the south coast, and among settlers on the nearby mainland.

Vincent Serventy

GLOSSARY

ambergris: literally means grey amber. A secretion in the intestines of the sperm whale used in making perfumes.

cess: short for success. Bad cess means bad luck to you.

crow's nest: a platform high up the mast of a ship where a person could rest while watching for whales, land or other objects.

daub: mud or clay; the boys used the word 'dab' but more often known as daub.

dodder laurel: a semi-parasitic twining plant with slender, yellowish stems and small round fruit.

easting: to sail to the east.

foot: ancient unit of measurement, probably the actual length of the foot of some long-gone king. Today, equal to approximately 30 centimetres; 0.3048 metres.

Fenians: Irish nationalists who opposed British rule of Ireland.

inch: a unit of measurement equal to approximately 2.5 centimetres; 25.4 millimetres.

klapmatch: a female seal.

lag: an old term for a convict sentenced to be transported to a penal colony.

leviathan: a huge sea monster.

mile: a unit of measurement, approximately 1.6 kilometres; 1609.34 metres.

paperbark: name of tree whose outer bark is thin and papery. Bark was used in earlier times for carrying food, or as a temporary roof for a hut.

pannikin: a metal drinking mug or cup, usually made of iron with a coating of tin.

pod: a group of animals, usually seals or whales.

pound: old measure of weight, approximately half a kilogram; 0.4536 kg. Also a unit of money, approximately 2 Australian dollars.

right whale: a large whale often hunted in earlier times because, when dead, the carcase floated instead of sinking, making this the 'right' whale to hunt.

sovereign: old gold coin once worth just over two dollars.

sperm whale: so called because of the 'spermaceti' in its head. This whitish, waxy substance was valued by whalers as it was used to make ointments and cosmetics.

tallow: hard fatty tissue from animals. Used for making candles and soap.

tammar: a small kind of wallaby found in south-western Australia and islands off the coast. It was the first marsupial reported by Europeans.

teal: a small kind of duck found over much of Australia.

ton: an old measure of weight, just over a modern tonne, approximately 1016 kg.

wig: a male seal.

zamia: a local plant resembling a palm but more ancient, being a cycad which looks like a cross between a fern and a palm. An important food for the Australian Aborigines but is poisonous if eaten without treatment.